D0952028

A QUESTION OF MOTIVE

A Selection of Recent Titles by Roderic Jeffries

AN AIR OF MURDER *
ARCADIAN DEATH
AN ARTISTIC WAY TO GO
DEFINITELY DECEASED *
AN ENIGMATIC DISAPPEARANCE
AN INSTINCTIVE SOLUTION *
AN INTRIGUING MURDER *
MURDER DELAYED *
MURDER'S LONG MEMORY
MURDER NEEDS IMAGINATION *
RELATIVELY DANGEROUS
SEEING IS DECEIVING *
A SUNNY DISAPPEARANCE *
SUN, SEA AND MURDER *
TOO CLEVER BY HALF

* *available from Severn House*

A QUESTION OF MOTIVE

Roderic Jeffries

This first world edition published 2009
in Great Britain and 2010 in the USA by
SEVERN HOUSE PUBLISHERS LTD of
9–15 High Street, Sutton, Surrey, England, SM1 1DF.
Trade paperback edition published
in Great Britain and the USA 2010 by
SEVERN HOUSE PUBLISHERS LTD

British Library Cataloguing in Publication Data

Jeffries, Roderic, 1926-
  A Question of Motive. – (An Inspector Alvarez mystery)
  1. Alvarez, Enrique (Fictitious character)–Fiction.
  2. Police–Spain–Majorca–Fiction. 3. English–Crimes
  against–Spain–Majorca–Fiction. 4. Detective and
  mystery stories.
  I. Title II. Series
  823.9'14-dc22

ISBN-13: 978-0-7278-6857-2   (cased)
ISBN-13: 978-1-84751-206-2   (trade paper)

All Severn House titles are printed on acid-free paper.

Severn House Publishers support The Forest Stewardship Council [FSC],
the leading international forest certification organisation. All our titles that
are printed on Greenpeace-approved FSC-certified paper carry the FSC logo.

Mixed Sources
Product group from well-managed
forests and other controlled sources
www.fsc.org Cert no. SA-COC-1565
© 1996 Forest Stewardship Council
FSC

Typeset by Palimpsest Book Production Ltd.,
Grangemouth, Stirlingshire, Scotland.
Printed and bound in Great Britain by
MPG Books Ltd., Bodmin, Cornwall

ONE

The end of the net dropped off the branch of one tree, causing the left hand to jerk free and the net to fall to the ground. Velaquez swore. He was losing his skill in setting up the thrush trap. Age stripped a man of everything. He crossed to the canvas satchel, brought out a bottle, and drank.

A distant sound – something snapping? – alarmed him and he prepared to act quickly and hide the net in the satchel, regaining the appearance of an honest man enjoying peace in the solitude of the woodland. Catching and eating thrushes had been declared illegal many years before but, like many Mallorquins, he regarded laws of little consequence unless they could not be evaded.

The sound was not repeated and he slowly relaxed. He drank more wine and brought a slice of pa amb oli – bread coated in olive oil and brushed with air-dried tomato – out of the rucksack.

Shafts of sunshine reached through the canopy of needle leaves, creating patterns on the rough, sparse undergrowth. A cicada shrilled, several replied and all became silent. He leaned his back against the trunk of a tree, lit a cigarette, buried the head of the used match in the ground. Fire was an ever-present danger with the undergrowth tinder dry. As he smoked, he noted any thrush on the wing which might suggest a flight path in which to set a net. He gazed briefly at the unusual, triangular outcrop of rock which ended in a sharp point. A century before, Ripoll, a halfwit, had insisted a giant had begun to carve himself a boat, but had found the rock too hard even for him and had given up. Derisively, the spur of rock had been called Ripoll's Barca, a name reduced in time to Barca.

When young, Velaquez, after a bet with Jorge, had tried to climb the steep wall of rock and had reached halfway before he had lost his grip and fallen, broken a leg. His mother had consoled him, his father had cursed him for incurring doctor's fees and Jorge had claimed the bet.

The top of Barca was flat – the foredeck? – before the land rose to a thousand metres – the accommodation and bridge? His father remembered the time when a retired Nationalist colonel had had a house built on the flat land. It had burned down in the mid forties of the previous century, some said through arson. The land, and the gutted house, had been put up for sale. Only a fool would buy it, was the local judgement. Eventually, that fool turned up. An Englishman who could judge the value of the site and with so much money he had built a grand house. Four bathrooms. What did one do with four? A swimming pool. When the sea was only seven kilometres away? A garden that had needed many, many lorry loads of imported earth and which grew nothing edible?

Velaquez stood. Jainta, his wife, wanted to be driven to Inca to see a friend who was ill. But before he left, he would spend a little time looking for thrushes on the other side of the Barca. He walked around the bows and stopped suddenly. Lying on the ground, his head battered, one arm outstretched, one under his body, lay a man.

Velaquez cursed his bad luck. He should report this, but to do so in person would cause the Policia Local to question why he was in the woods and they were unlikely to accept his reason that he enjoyed the peace. They would wonder if perhaps he was the man who had recently been selling forbidden thrushes to the villagers.

The duty officer picked up the receiver. 'Policia Local, Llueso.'

'There's a man lying on the ground at Barca.'

'Is he dead or injured?'

'Dead.'

'How can you be certain?'

'Because his head's like a squashed pomegranate.'

'Who is he?'

'I don't know.'

'Is there any ID on him?'
'Haven't looked.'
'Your name?'
The line became dead.

Alvarez drove slowly through the streets of Llueso, made even more narrow by badly parked cars, to his normal parking space. It was occupied by a car with French number plates. In an alternative space was an English-plated car. Foreigners' money might be necessary to the economy, but they weren't. He finally found a space, but this left him with a fifteen-minute walk through streets whose buildings trapped the breathless heat.

At the Guardia Civil post, the duty cabo pointed at the wall clock. Alvarez ignored the unnecessary indication that his siesta had been prolonged. He climbed the stairs, went into his office and slumped down on the chair behind the desk. Man was not made to work in such heat. Man was not made to work.

The telephone rang and he stared at it with sharp dislike. It might mistakenly be called one of the benefits of modern civilization; in truth, it was a bane.

'Enrique, Felipe Oller here. Long time, no see, so how's the world treating you?'

'It never does.'

'As cheerful as ever! I saw Dolores a few days ago, but there wasn't time for a chat. Young Juan must be quite a lad now. And Isabel will be having her first communion . . . By the way, I'm calling to say there's a report of a body of a man at the foot of Barca. Do you know where that is?'

'You think I'm from Barcelona?'

'Seems he fell from up top and landed on his head.'

'What's the victim's name?'

'No idea.'

'Who reported it?'

'Anonymous.'

'You've confirmation of the report?'

'No.'

'Then it's maybe a hoax.'

'Which is why you'll need to check.'

'It's your job to do that. It'll have been an accident.'

'Who's to say? Years ago, soon after I started here, a young unmarried woman who was in bud threw herself off Barca because in those days she'd have been held in contempt by everyone when she popped it.'

'Men don't become pregnant.'

'A word of warning. Our new sergeant is a pocket Napoleon. If he thinks you're trying to skive, he'll create trouble.'

'Skive? All I'm making certain is that the right procedure is observed.'

'And I believe in mermaids.'

Resentfully, Alvarez replaced the receiver. People were becoming ever less ready to work.

TWO

It was many years since Alvarez had last seen Barca, yet nothing had changed. The tourist tsunami had not wreaked its havoc. No unsightly huddle of flats and houses was in sight.

He rounded the spur and saw the body. The telephone call had not been a hoax. As he approached it, he tried and failed to overcome the harsh reminder that to live was to die, sometimes violently.

The damage to the head made it difficult to judge age and appearance, but guesswork suggested early sixties. The dead man wore a white cotton shirt, white shorts, good-quality sandals. The shirt label recorded it had been made in England; in a pocket of the shorts was a note on which was written, in English: 3 AAA batteries, mobile, *Telegraph*. The victim was probably English.

There was nothing to do until the doctor and photographer turned up, so he settled on the ground. Relaxation was a stressed man's therapy.

Jurando was the first to arrive. He gave Alvarez a cheerful greeting – an unusual doctor – briefly referred to the last time they had met and asked after Alvarez's family. He put a small bag down on the ground, studied the body from a distance. 'What do you know about him?'

'Nothing. The policia received an anonymous phone call to say there was a body here and I decided to come and check, rather than leave it to them. I had a brief search for identification, naturally taking care to disturb as little as possible, and there's good reason to believe him to be English.'

'Right. I'll see what information I can add.' Jurando opened his bag and brought out a pair of surgeon's gloves and a forensic thermometer. He crossed to the body, walked slowly around it, bent down and began his examination.

Watching, Alvarez was saddened by the irrational thought that death could strip a man of all his dignity.

Jurando returned, put gloves in a disposable plastic bag, thermometer in a clinical holder and returned both to his case. He stood. 'Injuries are consistent with a fall from some height.' He scratched the lobe of his right ear. 'There are signs of bruising on his stomach.

'I suppose you'll want a time of death, even though this will be as unreliable as ever. Rigor is in the face, jaw, and neck muscles, but not in arms and legs; together with the body temperature, this suggests roughly six hours ago.'

Alvarez looked at his watch; death had been at around 1300 hours.

'From here, there's no sign of fencing above. If there is some, which surely there must be, it's set well back, so it's unlikely he was on the wrong side by chance. A possible suicide?'

'More likely he'd been drinking and forgot where he was.'

'PM results will answer that one. You can arrange for the body to be collected and taken to the morgue. And if you'd let them know I'll hope to carry out the PM at midday tomorrow.'

Jurando left, his walk as brisk as when he had arrived. Alvarez lit a cigarette. It was depressing to witness such energy in a man of roughly his own age. Perhaps he really should give up smoking and drink less.

He used his mobile to ask for the body to be collected. 'And will you tell . . .'

'Hang on. Where d'you say it is?'

'At the foot of Barca.'

'Is that a hotel?'

It was extraordinary how ignorant people could be. He explained how to drive to the rock.

Cuesta, a commercial photographer with a contract to carry out police work, arrived as Alvarez switched off the mobile. They discussed village matters and their respective families before Cuesta walked over to the body. 'Careless, leaving this mess for someone else to clear up!'

A crude, heartless remark, said to try to lessen a sense of shocked revulsion. 'What shots do you want?'

'General, close-ups of the head, and some of the cliff face.'

He watched Cuesta work with practised skill. Cuesta had been born, and for several years had lived, in Mestara, which had explained his initial problem in enjoying a successful business in Llueso. However, when it had become obvious he was far more skilful than his only competitor, his work had greatly increased. Then the rumour had spread that he was asking women and older girls to let him photograph them in the nude. Even after he had been able to show the falsity of the accusation, fostered by his rival, it had been a long time before a woman of good reputation would enter his studio unaccompanied by family or friend. As many said, no bonfire burned unless a match had been put to it.

Cuesta crossed to where Alvarez stood. 'That's done. Do you know what happened?'

'Not yet.'

'Any idea when he died?'

'According to Doctor Jurando, at about thirteen hundred hours.'

'Was it likely suicide?'

'I doubt it.' Suicide meant it became his case; accident was the policia's problem.

THREE

Alvarez looked at his watch, hoping it was time for *merienda*. Since he had only recently arrived at the post, he was not surprised to find it was not. Yet a coffee and coñac before he phoned Salas would have provided welcome insulation.

There was a time when a man could find no way of avoiding what a man had to do. He picked up the receiver, dialled, and almost immediately Señorita Torres, Salas' secretary, said: 'Superior Chief Salas' office.'

'Inspector Alvarez, speaking from Llueso.'

'What is it?'

Her tone had been even less welcoming than usual. 'Is Superior Chief Salas in his office?'

'Naturally.'

There was nothing natural in working on a Saturday morning when one was senior enough not to. 'I have to make a report.'

'Wait.'

He had not opened the morning post. As he balanced the receiver against neck and shoulder, he checked through the unopened letters to see if there was an envelope with an official appearance which might mean Salas would refer to it.

'Yes?'

No good morning, no query about his health, but then Salas was a Madrileño. 'Señor, yesterday morning, the local police received a report of the finding of a dead man . . .'

'The identity of the informer?'

'I can't answer that because . . .'

'The identity of the dead man?'

'I don't know because . . .'

'It will greatly shorten this report if you record what, if anything, you do know.'

'The information was that the body was by Barca . . .'

'Am I being unduly optimistic to hope you can name the boat?'

'It isn't one. It's a rock in the foothills of the Serra de Tramuntana, not all that far from Llueso.'

'By what logic do you refer to a rock as a boat?'

'Years ago, a man bereft of full intelligence thought a giant had been trying to carve out a boat, but had found the task too tough even for him and he got no further than forming the bows and foredeck . . . If that is the right terminology?'

'I am as uninterested in boats as I am in giants.'

'I was trying to explain . . .'

'And failing. So before you introduce a flying carpet, try to give a lucid report.'

'Following a call from the Policia Local in Llueso, I drove as far as possible and then walked to Barca. There was a body on the far side of the rock. It seemed obvious he had fallen, landing on his head, from the top of Barca. I called Doctor Jurando – he has forensic qualifications – who said the injuries were consistent with a fall. Death would have been instantaneous. Doctor Jurando provided an estimate of the time of death, adding the usual proviso. It was at about one, yesterday afternoon.'

'You are aware that today is Saturday?'

'Yes, señor. But the body was not reported until late yesterday afternoon and by the time I had confirmed this was not a hoax, the doctor had made his examination, the photographer had finished, and it was too late to report to you.'

'Why?'

'You would have returned home.'

'A presumption no doubt based on your times of work. Has it occurred to you to determine the cause of the fall?'

'It was probably an accident.'

'You would like to explain why?'

'Someone in the house . . .'

'What house?'

'The one on Barca.'

'Is it your intention to make your report more interesting by initially ignoring facts and then introducing them one by one, forcing the listener constantly to guess where they might lead?'

'Although it is the mountainous area, at Barca there is relatively flat land of about one and a half hectares. Rather a strange feature is . . .'

'You will forgo the suggestion it was created by the giant stamping his foot in anger at his inability to complete the boat.'

'There is a large house on the flat land. The original one was built by a colonel, but this was unfortunately burned down, some said . . .'

'The history may be of interest to anyone who has the time to listen to it, I do not.'

'It's my guess that the victim is someone from the house, unaware of, or oblivious to, the danger of getting too close to the edge of the cliff.'

'You would not expect that the circumstances would have been reported long before the unknown man discovered the body? And why have you not taken the trouble to determine whether, in fact, the victim is from the house?'

'I will be doing so when I finish my report, señor.'

'I presume you have failed to consider suicide?'

'On the contrary.'

'But since you have not yet troubled to identify the victim, any judgement – including that of accident – is without credibility.'

'There was no note of intended suicide on the victim.'

'You disregard the possibility that such a note was left in the house.'

'In my experience . . .'

'We will stick with facts. You will ascertain what these are and then report to me. And since I have important work to complete, I shall be here, in my office, until late tonight and for much of tomorrow. I do not, therefore, expect to be informed on Monday morning that you were unable to contact me.'

Alvarez replaced the receiver. He had hoped to leave the

investigation to the policia local, but initially, at any rate, he was going to have to conduct it.

He opened the bottom right-hand drawer of the desk and brought out a half-full bottle of 504 and a glass, was about to pour a drink when he remembered his promise to reduce his drinking. He hesitated. The promise was to reduce, not prohibit.

Fifteen minutes later, he left the post and walked to Club Llueso for his delayed *merienda*.

Without being asked, Roca, the bartender, poured out a brandy and a café cortado, and brought them to the end of the bar.

Alvarez raised the glass and studied the depth of brandy. 'Short measure again.'

'So give me the glass and I'll pour you a standard measure.'

He drank.

FOUR

The drive up to the top of Barca was relatively short, but for Alvarez, an altophobe, it was panic-inducing. The road, a minor example of the Spanish ability to overcome 'impossible' terrain, climbed the side of the rock face with two sharp bends which had no safety barrier on the outside. A car could fall over the side far too easily – an unintended twitch of the wheel would be sufficient. His hands had seemed constantly about to twitch.

Previously, he had only seen the house – more accurately, parts of it – from below and he had been unable to appreciate it possessed a graceful form which could suggest an Italian architect. Externally attractive houses were not a common sight on the island; old ones had been built for permanence, modern ones were often a clutter of different roof levels and inharmonious lines. It complemented its site. Its height provided it with a sweeping view of pine trees, farmland, Port Llueso, the bay with its travel-poster-blue waters, the backdrop of mountains, the nature reserve to the east . . .

'Do you want something?'

To Alvarez, the speaker's tone had suggested he thought the visitor might be trying to sell something. Alvarez turned. Standing in the doorway was a man in his early thirties, carefully handsome, dressed in a spotless, uncreased white shirt and black, sharply creased trousers.

'To speak to the owner of the house.'

'You are?'

'Inspector Alvarez, Cuerpo General de Policia.'

'Oh! . . . I'm sorry, Inspector, but I didn't realize who you were.'

'Perhaps because we've never met. The owner's name?'

'Señor Gill.'

'He is here?'

'I'm afraid he is away, Inspector. Is something wrong?'

He ignored the question. 'Is there any member of the family here?'

'Señorita Farren, the señor's niece.'

'Who else?'

'Luisa, my wife, and Eva, the maid. Santos is the gardener.'

'Your name is?'

'Parra.'

'You work around the house?' Alvarez asked, convinced Parra would prefer to be thought of as the butler.

'I am lucky enough to do so, yes.'

There was no need to be fulsome. A Mallorquin was the equal of anyone, even if he swept the streets. 'I'll speak to her.'

'Will you please come this way, Inspector?'

He entered a spacious hall and waited as Parra opened a door, stepped inside and said: 'Inspector Alvarez wishes to speak to you, señorita, if it is convenient.'

'Please ask him to come in, Pablo.'

Mary Farren was dressed with the casual elegance money could provide. Her rich, auburn hair held a natural wave, her eyes were dark blue, her nose graceful, her lips firmly shaped. But on the left-hand side of her jaw, harmony was lost in heavy scarring and a slight, but noticeable, misshapen line.

'Please sit,' she said in heavily accented Spanish.

'Thank you, señorita,' he answered in English. The chair cosseted him with expensive luxury.

'Before we go any further, may I offer you coffee or a drink?'

'A drink would be very welcome.'

'Will you tell Pablo what you would like?'

Parra had remained just inside the doorway.

'A coñac with just ice, please,' he said in Mallorquin.

'And I will have a Dubonnet.'

Parra left and closed the door.

'How can I help you, Inspector?' she asked.

It seemed from the lack of any suggestion of alarm, any understanding of why he might be there, they had not heard about the dead body at the foot of Barca. He had to try to learn the facts without alarming her unless, or until, that became necessary. 'I understand you employ Parra, his wife, a maid and a gardener?'

'I assure you that we pay all the appropriate taxes.'

'I would not doubt that, señorita. Is there anyone else who works here?'

'Eloisa, but only when we have a party. She comes in and helps out.'

'Have you any guests staying at the moment?'

'No, why are you asking these questions?'

'I will explain in a moment. Do the servants live in their own quarters?'

'Yes. That is, except for Santos. He owns a finca between Llueso and Port Llueso, so he doesn't need accommodation.' She stopped. After a moment, she continued: 'Last year he did think it would be a good idea if the family moved into the two empty staff rooms because he wouldn't be tired out by travelling to and fro and he could work longer.'

He was unable to resist the comment: 'An unusual wish!'

She smiled. 'We imagined he was hoping to have the chance to let his finca to tourists during the summer. But for us, three children under eight would have destroyed all peace.'

Parra returned, a silver salver in his hand. He crossed to where she sat, placed a glass on the piecrust table by her side, added a small bowl. 'The cheese sticks you like.'

'Well remembered! Will you see if the inspector would like some?'

Parra put a glass and the bowl down for Alvarez. 'Is that all, señorita?'

'Yes, thank you.'

He left.

She raised her glass. 'Your health.'

They drank. Alvarez had been hoping for a good brandy and was not disappointed. Carlos III?

'Inspector, you were going to explain the reason for your questions.'

'Please allow me to ask a few more, señorita, before I do so. Parra told me Señor Gill is not here. That is so?'

'Yes. Have you tried the cheese straws?'

'Not yet, I fear.' He picked out two, held them in his left hand, carried the bowl over to her. She thanked him as he returned to his seat. 'Can you say where he is?'

'Probably. Why do you want to know that? And please don't say you'll explain later on. You're making me very worried that he's in some sort of trouble.'

Did he prevaricate further? If he did, her fear could be exacerbated rather than held in check. 'Clearly, señorita, you have not learned that the body of a man was found below Barca this morning.'

'My God!'

'If I know where Señor Gill is, I can speak to him.'

'But he doesn't . . . You can't think it may be he.'

She had spoken with certainty, not alarm. 'I have no knowledge who is the unfortunate man. Therefore, I have to consider he may have come from your house. When did you last see your uncle?'

'When I left to go to Palma yesterday morning.'

'You have not seen him today?' Her answers confused him. 'Were you aware he was not here this morning?'

'When he didn't come down to breakfast, I went up to his room and saw his bed had not been slept in.'

'That must have worried you?'

After a long silence, she said in a low voice: 'No, it didn't.'

'Why is that?'

'Because he had obviously gone to see a friend and stayed the night.'

'He often does so?'

'When . . .'

'Yes, señorita?'

'Do you have to know?'

'I think so.'

'It's so complicated.'

He waited.

'Robin's wife died some years ago. Then last year we

were invited to a party at which we met the Oakleys. He . . .
he became friendly with Virginia.'

'And is with her now?'

'He'd have let me know if he wasn't. You see . . . He
must know I can guess how the relationship is, but if it's
not put into words . . .'

'You can speak to Señora Oakley and ask if he is there?'

'I suppose so . . . But it will embarrass both of them. And
me.'

'Nevertheless, I think I must ask you to get in touch.'

She hesitated, finally stood, crossed to the telephone which
stood on a rosewood card table. She lifted the receiver, dialled,
listened, replaced the receiver. He assumed she had dialled the
wrong number.

'He . . . he's not there.'

'How can you be certain?'

'Paul answered.'

'He is the husband?'

'Robin must have gone to stay with friends in Andraitx.
He's repeatedly said he hadn't seen them for a long time and
must do so.' She spoke intently. 'That's where he must be.'

'Would you please ring them.'

She might not have heard him. He watched her changing
expressions and was convinced he could correctly interpret
them because he had known a time when logic said one thing,
the heart another. When he had been told Juana-María had
been crushed against a wall by a drunken French driver, he
had driven at a reckless speed to the hospital, knowing her
injuries must be very serious, praying that she was not badly
hurt because the car had been moving slowly, she would smile
at him and the doctor would say she would be fit and well
in a short time. She had died minutes after he reached her in
intensive care. 'Please, señorita, speak to them.'

She stood, crossed to the card table, picked up a small
tabulated notebook. She opened this at the wrong page,
finally found what she wanted, went to dial, but stopped.
'I . . . I can't.' Her voice shook. 'You'll have to.'

He walked over and took the notebook from her. 'Which
name is it?'

'Green.'

He dialled.

'Yes?'

'May I speak to Señor Gill, please?'

'I'm afraid he's not here.'

'I am sorry to have troubled you.' He replaced the receiver before he could be asked why he was phoning. 'He's not with them, señorita.'

'Then he's with the Yates. Or the Keens,' she said wildly.

'Before I speak to them, I must have a word with Parra.'

'I tell you, he has to be with one of them.'

'Please believe me, it will be best if I talk to Parra first.'

She mumbled something. Fear raised lines in her face.

He crossed to her chair and put a hand on her shoulder. 'Courage, señorita . . .'

She jerked his hand off with a quick shrug. 'Don't,' she cried shrilly.

'But . . .'

'Don't touch me.'

He was bewildered. 'I was trying to offer you comfort. We Mallorquins often touch each other as a mark of comfort, sympathy, friendship. I fear I had forgotten that many do not regard this in the same way.'

She made a sound like a strangled cry, stood, walked to the window and stared out. When she spoke, her voice was strained. 'I . . . I couldn't help myself because . . .'

'There is no need to explain.'

'I must.'

About to repeat what he had just said, he checked the words. Why, was difficult to explain, but he was certain that by explaining the reason for her apparent gauche action, she would in some way lessen the panicky fear which gripped her. He could remember how, as he drove into the grounds of the hospital where Juana-María lay, he had promised himself he would forgo much if she recovered. It had been as if he had believed his self-sacrifice could help her.

'Three years ago . . . Three years ago, I was returning from work in the City. I left the tube at Ealing and walked up the road, as I did every evening. There was a house on a corner which was empty and for sale. The front garden had a hedge around it. I was passing the gate when a man came out from the garden, put an arm around my throat, and dragged me inside. I fought, chewed his hand and made him let me go, screamed for help. He cursed me, threw me to the ground, kicked me in the face and side, and ran. I kept screaming and a couple found me and called for help.

'I was six weeks in hospital. When I came out, I was terrified if a man I didn't know very well tried to touch me. I've tried and tried to cure myself and failed. I simply couldn't stop myself shouting at you even though it was absurdly rude.'

'It is kind of you to have explained.'

'You looked so dismayed.'

And now he would have to ask more questions which would possibly bring her fresh tragedy. 'As I mentioned, I need to have a word with Parra.'

She looked at him with sharp worry.

He left the sitting room, searched for and found the kitchen. Parra stood by the central table. Luisa Parra, as he presumed she must be, was stirring a pot on one of the gas rings set on top of an electric oven.

She stopped stirring and turned. 'You're the inspector?'

'That's right.' Older than Parra, she possessed none of her husband's sleek looks. Her figure said that she enjoyed much of her own cooking.

Cooks demanded praise. Alvarez said: 'What you're preparing smells delicious.'

'Fabada Asturiana as it should be made.'

'A dish for the gods!' He turned to Parra. 'Can you say when you last saw the señor?'

'Yesterday morning before we left for our day off.' He spoke to his wife. 'Was it around ten o'clock?'

'A quarter past.'

'You spoke to him then?' Alvarez asked.

'Only to say we were leaving,' Parra answered.

'Did you know he was going out?'

'He had said he wouldn't be here for lunch so there was no need to leave him a meal.'

'And the señorita was not eating here?'

'She was going to Palma to do some shopping and might eat there or return to one of the local restaurants.'

'Is the señor's car in the garage?'

'I imagine not.'

'Will you find out, please?'

'You think he may have been in some sort of accident?'

'At the moment, I don't think anything for certain.'

Parra left and quickly returned. 'His car is still there. Someone must have picked him up.'

'I want a photograph of him. Find one if you can.'

'I'll ask the señorita . . .'

'No.'

'But . . .'

'It will be best if she does not learn I have asked. Obviously, neither of you has heard a man was found dead at the foot of Barca, having fallen from the top.'

She turned, holding a wooden spoon, and stared at Alvarez. 'Sweet Mary!'

'It might be the señor?' Parra asked.

'It is a possibility.'

Parra spoke to his wife. 'Didn't I tell him?'

'More than once,' she answered.

'And he was annoyed and told me he was capable of managing his own life without my assistance?'

'I heard him say that.'

'What did you tell him which so annoyed him?' Alvarez asked.

'That when he warned everyone not to go beyond the fencing, it was stupid of him to do so. Not, of course, that I used the word "stupid".'

'You have seen him step over the fencing?'

'Many times.'

'Recently?'

'Happens several times a week.'

'Why would he take such a risk?'

'To check or photograph the orchid.'

'Orchid?'

'It's growing between the fencing and the edge of the cliff.'

'Wouldn't have thought anything would grow on the rock.'

'It's in a gully filled with muck. Some time back a friend was staying here and noticed it. He said it was rare and had never been seen before so far away from its natural habitat or in so inhospitable a place. It was such a rarity, the señor had to do everything he could to protect it. It was called Mosques . . .' He stopped.

'Mosques blanques,' she said.

'He was very interested in flowers?' Alvarez asked.

'Used to be that he just liked them in the garden.'

'Funny thing to get interested in.'

'I suppose it's because it's so rare. And he said it was so beautiful.'

Beauty was a personal judgement. 'Perhaps you'd find a photo of him?'

'I'll see what I can do.' Parra left.

Luisa moved a saucepan on to an unlit burner and switched off the gas. 'The dead man may be the señor?'

'Until I see a photo of him, I won't know.'

'But you think it is him?'

He did not answer her question directly. 'Has he seemed very depressed recently?'

'Why do you ask?'

'Has he?'

'Wouldn't have said so.'

'He was the same as usual?'

'The little I saw of him.'

Parra returned to the kitchen and handed Alvarez a framed photograph of Gill and a woman.

'Who is she?'

'His late wife.'

Despite the injuries to the head of the dead man, there could be no doubt.

'Is it him?' Parra asked.

'Yes.'

Luisa said something incomprehensible.

'I must tell her,' Parra said.

'I will,' Alvarez contradicted.

'Wouldn't it be kinder since she knows me?'

'It is going to be cruel whoever tells her and it is my duty to do so.'

'Please be gentle,' Luisa said.

'Of course. If you come with me, you will be able to offer her what I cannot.'

She spoke to her husband. 'Watch the fabada.'

They went through to the sitting room. Mary stood by the right-hand picture window. She swung round, looked briefly at Luisa, then at Alvarez.

He spoke directly, convinced this was the kindest thing to do. 'Señorita, I am very sorry to have to tell you it was your uncle who fell.'

Her lips trembled and her face contorted. 'No. Please God, he can't be dead.'

Luisa went forward and put her arms around Mary.

He returned to the kitchen. If Parra was keeping close watch on the cooking, this was not immediately apparent since he was seated at the table.

'How did she . . .' Parra stopped.

'As one must expect. Your wife is consoling her. I need to know something concerning the señor.'

'I know nothing about his private life.'

'I wouldn't expect you to. What has his behaviour been like in the past few days? Has he been acting normally?'

'Yes.'

'He wasn't depressed?'

'I suppose he wasn't as cheerful as most times and maybe a bit down and a shade short-tempered.'

'Your wife thinks he was very normal.'

'She doesn't see him nearly as much as I do.'

'Any idea why he could have been depressed?'

'Might have been money.'

'Why d'you say that?'

'He complained to Luisa that housekeeping was becoming increasingly expensive and maybe there'd have to be cuts in things like lobster.'

'That's all?'

'Well . . . I did happen to hear him speaking on the

telephone because I was passing through the room. Couldn't help hearing. You understand?'

'You wouldn't wish to be thought eavesdropping. Why is what he said of interest?'

'It seemed he could have lost a lot of money in the financial crisis.'

'Could or had?'

'Wasn't in the room long enough to hear.'

Alvarez asked further questions but learned nothing fresh. He left the house and noticed a man working on a flower bed. In contrast to the normal form of weeding – dragging, chopping, chipping the earth with a mattock, to the detriment of flowers as well as weeds – he was kneeling and using a hand-fork. He stood as Alvarez approached.

'Are you Santos?'

'And you're from the cuerpo.'

Alvarez made a brief judgement. Moorish blood many generations back, a rugged face, broad mouth, strong shoulders, and a self-possessed manner which said he considered himself at least the equal of the next man. 'You know what's happened?'

'Been told there's a dead man below.'

'I'm afraid it may be the señor.'

'Can't say I'm surprised.'

'Why's that?'

'Would go over the fencing to look at that bloody orchid. Said he wanted to record it for his friend. If it hadn't been there, he'd never have been so daft.'

'Did he often step over the fencing to look at it?'

'Near every day.'

'Did you see him on Saturday?'

'No.'

'When did you knock off work?'

'Midday, same as ever.'

'Will you show me where the orchid is.'

They walked across the lawn to the four-bar fencing, a metre high, uprights set in concrete, which imaged the curve of the rock, two metres back from it. When they came to a stop, Alvarez faced the edge of the cliff and the emptiness beyond. Although he could accept he was in no danger, already he was breathing more quickly than usual, there was tension in his stomach, objects seen in the corners of his eyes seemed to ripple, and soon he knew a sirens' song would call on him to walk up to the edge and over.

'Something wrong, you're walking so slowly?' Santos asked.

'A touch of lumbago,' he answered, unwilling to admit to his handicap. 'Where is it?'

'Straight in front of you.'

Over decades, the cleft in the rock face had become filled with dust, needle leaves and airborne debris, providing a small bed of 'soil'. In the centre, grew the single Mosques blanques. Since it had caused so much interest, he had expected something large and brilliantly colourful. He saw a small, single green stem, three unopened lips and three opened ones which displayed tongues in shades of brown and blue and indeterminate white edges. 'Doesn't look worth all the effort,' was his spoken judgement.

'You need to look at it real close. Hop over the fence and get your head down and then see what you think.'

'I'll stay here.'

'The señor must have got so busy with the photos, he momentarily forgot where he was and stepped too far back,' Santos said.

'Might have been like that. Only . . .' Alvarez stopped.

'What?'

'There's obviously no camera up here, and there wasn't one down below.'

'So you're thinking?' Santos demanded angrily.

Alvarez shrugged his shoulders.

'Wondering if I pinched it, ain't you?'

'No.'

'Likely don't trust even yourself. Then have a think on this. He often went to look at the plant without photographing it. And if you think I'm lying, ask the others. They've seen him.'

'I was merely remarking the fact.'

'I could remark about you lot, only it'd take too long.'

'You misjudge us.'

Santos expressed his opinion of that.

'Calm down and have a smoke.' Alvarez brought a pack of cigarettes out of the pocket of his trousers.

'Giving something away? Must be wanting more than you're offering,' he said as he withdrew a cigarette.

Alvarez lit a match for them both. He stared out at the world below. 'I call this a slice of heaven!'

'It maybe for you seeing as you don't have to work, but it ain't for me.'

'If I lived in Aguila . . .'

'You wouldn't be in the cuerpo, sticking your nose into other people's lives.'

'Did the señor own any of the land below?'

'Fifty hectares.'

'What did he do with it?'

'Nothing. Said it was wonderful to be able to preserve the land as it's been since ever. Daft. It would be worth millions of euros with building permission.'

'Which wouldn't be given.'

'You're in the cuerpo and never learned about brown envelopes?'

'This far back from the coast, there wouldn't be enough encouragement money to get the politicians interested . . . Like I said, it's perfect. You can see the sea, but you're too far away to have the tourists causing trouble.'

'You reckon? There was an article in some book or magazine mentioning the Barca and how it was supposed to happen, so now we have people coming to gawp. The señor didn't worry – strange man, seemed to think it'd help them to learn to like nature, or something like that. Never said anything provided they wasn't carving names on trees or leaving rubbish. Only thing that really pissed him off was the man he kept seeing who he was certain was poaching birds, after he found a bit of netting caught up on a tree. Tried to catch him at it. And maybe one day did. I was up here and could hear him below having a right row with someone; he spoke Spanish, the other bloke, Mallorquin. Doubt the señor understood what he was being called.'

'The argument was heated?'

'Bloody loud.'

'He thought the poacher was after what – thrushes?'

'Always plenty of 'em below.'

'Who was the poacher?'

'Can't say.'

'Why not?'

'Never seen him, that's why.'

'Yet you heard him. You didn't recognize his voice?'

'No.'

Santos spoke with such emphasis that Alvarez wondered if the poacher was a friend of his.

FIVE

Alvarez turned into Carrer Conte Rossi – renamed in honour of an Italian fascist; the consequences of the Civil War had long lingered – to find there was no space in front of No. 8. Years ago, no sensible person would have parked in front of a home known to be inhabited by a member of the cuerpo. Sadly, democracy diluted authority.

He walked slowly along the pavement since heat and exertion could be fatal. At No. 8, he stepped into the entrada which, as always, was in immaculate condition. Dust was unknown, the upright chairs with leather backs and seats of criss-crossed flax were geometrically placed, the table was covered with a newly ironed white embroidered linen cloth, patterned in blue flowers with wide petals, and the indoor plants had been wiped down.

In the sitting/dining room, Jaime was seated, morosely staring at the bare table.

'Not drinking?' Alvarez asked as he sat. 'Decided to become TT?'

Jaime jerked his head in the direction of the bead curtain across the open kitchen doorway, where his wife was cooking.

'She's forgotten to buy some?'

'Says we're better without it.'

'Is she . . .' He stopped abruptly as Dolores came through the curtain.

'I do not intend to spend all morning in a kitchen which is hotter than the devil's breath because my husband will not mend the fan, cooking a meal when he and my cousin will have drunk so much that they cannot say whether they are eating pastel de pollo con jamón or pollo insipido.'

'You don't understand.'

'I understand when a man finds it difficult to put a forkful of food into his mouth at the first attempt.'

'I've had a hell of a morning,' Alvarez said.

'Then you are able to appreciate how every morning of every week is for me.'

'I'm exhausted.'

'You stopped at too many bars on your way here?'

'I hurried straight back in order not to be late and upset your cooking.'

'Would you also like me to believe you have seen fairies dancing in the old square?'

'As a matter of fact, when I came through it yesterday, there were two men . . .'

'Enough!' She withdrew.

'Get the coñac out,' Alvarez said in a low voice.

Jaime stared uneasily at the bead curtain.

He should never have allowed Dolores to behave in so imperious a manner, Alvarez told himself. From the day of their marriage, Jaime had needed to make it very clear he was the jefe and he would decide when he would drink, she would not.

Jaime reached over and opened a door of the Mallorquin sideboard, brought out a bottle of Soberano and two glasses. Despite his unspoken advice to Jaime, Alvarez poured carefully and quietly, not wishing to alert Dolores.

Jaime brought a packet of Pall Mall out of his pocket, offered Alvarez a cigarette and struck a match for them both. 'What's gone so wrong with your morning?'

'I had to identify a body by Barca.'

'Who was it?'

'Señor Gill.'

'Never heard of him. He sounds foreign so why get bothered?'

'I had to tell the niece what had happened. And she . . .'

'Killed herself on a bonfire like they used to in India?'

'Was very distressed.'

'Why?'

'I've just said.'

'But if he was just an uncle?'

'At a guess, the relationship was more like father and daughter.'

'How old is she?'

'Early to mid twenties.'

'Attractive?'

'Apart from an old facial injury.'

'All the right bits and bobs?'

'I suppose.'

'You didn't notice?'

'I was trying to console her, not size her up.'

'How did the consoling go?'

Dolores stepped through the bead curtain. 'Are you ready to eat, or would a meal be a hindrance to your drinking?'

'I've hardly touched my glass,' Jaime complained.

'You also have seen fairies dancing in the square?'

Alvarez settled on his chair in the office. He picked up the receiver, replaced it, finally picked it up again and dialled.

'Superior Chief Salas' office,' Angela Torres said, in tones of assumed authority.

'I should like to speak to the superior chief, señorita.'

'Who is calling?'

She knew very well. 'Inspector Alvarez.'

'Wait.'

He had met her once. One might have called her passably attractive in a mature sense were her features not so sharp. She was unmarried because there was ice inside her. There was warmth inside Mary Farren, but she was unmarried perhaps because of her appearance, probably from past emotional distress. Did either of them consider spinsterhood to be a misfortune? Dolores complained that a married woman's misfortune was her husband.

The silence ceased when Salas said: 'Well?'

'Good afternoon, señor.'

'I have been expecting to hear from you for a long time.'

'There was difficulty in identifying the dead man.'

'Which deceased man?'

'Señor Gill.'

'Who is he?'

'He was found at the foot of Barca . . .'

'Alvarez, did any of your ancestors live in Boeotia?'

'I doubt it.'

'The inhabitants of Central Greece were noted for their limited intelligence. When one reports to a senior officer, who is occupied by many cases, his burden is eased by initially identifying about what and whom the report concerns. Clearly, you have no wish to ease my burden, as great as you manage to make it.'

There was a silence.

'You don't understand what I have just said?'

'I didn't go into many details, señor, because I thought you would know what I have been doing.'

'I am seldom given such opportunity.'

'I received a report that a dead man was lying at the foot of Barca. That is the name given to a wedge of rock by a man of small understanding. Perhaps his father had been born in Boeotia.'

'You consider that comment to be witty?'

'No, señor.'

'Then continue your report without unnecessary comments and repetitions.'

'The dead man had fallen from above, so it seemed reasonable to think he had been living, or had been staying, in Aquila, the house on top.'

'The home of Prometheus.'

'No. Señor Gill.'

'Why did he fall?'

'It could be because he was looking at the orchid and in a moment of forgetfulness, stepped back too far.'

'It pleases you to speak nonsense?'

'The orchid apparently is of considerable importance. An expert said it was rare and needed to be carefully looked after. Señor Gill seems to have become fascinated by it and was often examining or photographing it. To do this, he had to climb over the fence and remain on a ledge of rock which is far from wide. It was a silly thing to do, however rare the orchid, and even though the señor obviously did not suffer from altophobia.'

'You are referring to the so-called fear of heights?'

'Yes, señor.'

'A lack of mental discipline.'

'It's not like that.'

'I did not request an opinion.'

'But it's beyond control. Even a small height can cause the phobia, however much one tells oneself one is not afraid; there is mind-numbing fear, yet one suffers the urge to approach the edge as if sirens are singing to draw one on . . .'

'If the mind is numbed, it will not hear singing. Have you thought to confirm if he actually did ever step voluntarily over the guard barrier?'

'The gardener, the cook and her husband, have seen him do so frequently.'

'Then the facts indicate accident.'

'I have learned the señor may have suffered financial problems.'

'Far from unique. I bought shares in a company because a friend swore they were bound to appreciate and they have depreciated heavily.'

'Señor Gill told Luisa . . .'

'Who?'

'The cook.'

'What did she tell the señor?'

'It's the other way round.'

'You sow confusion like a spinner. Would you explain who said what to whom.'

'Luisa was to cut the cost of housekeeping. And Parra, her husband, overheard a telephone call which suggested the señor had lost money in the financial chaos.'

'So has everyone else.'

'But if he . . .'

'Why couldn't the damn fools have seen what was happening?'

'I suppose, like everyone else . . .'

'Everyone else has not bought shares which have fallen out of sight.'

There was silence.

'You have nothing more to add?' Salas asked.

'Not before I speak to the señorita and try to find out how much capital the señor lost.'

'Everything, judging by what I have suffered . . . What's your conclusion?'

'It could have been suicide or an accident.'

'You have not found any suicide note?'

'No, but not every man about to commit suicide writes down his intention.'

'Did you not suggest that it could not have been suicide because there was no note?'

'That was before I learned he had shown signs of depression.'

'And long before I have been allowed to learn that. Had he consulted a doctor?'

'I very much doubt it.'

'Then why do you say he may have been depressed?'

'Parra, the man who works in the house and is . . .'

'I am well aware of his identity.'

'He thought the señor had become less cheerful, short-tempered, and shown signs of depression. His wife disagreed, but she saw the señor far less often than her husband did.'

'Have you spoken to the señorita to learn her impression?'

'Not yet.'

'Why not?'

'She is very emotionally distressed and it will be kinder not to trouble her at the moment.'

'The investigation is to wait until you decide she is sufficiently recovered?'

'When she is, her answers are more likely to be correct.'

'If you are asking the questions, that possibility seems remote.'

Alvarez drove down to the port and along the front road towards Playa Neuva, stopped when halfway along. The beauty of the deep-blue sea, scarcely rippled by the lightest of breezes so that only a few optimists were out with wind-surfers, and the grandeur of the mountains which ringed the bay, provided him with the sense of peace and contentment they could offer to someone responsive to their beauty.

When trouble was everywhere and hope had been shredded, he would retire to the bay and slowly trouble would disperse and hope would return.

Reluctantly, he left and drove to Aquila. The road leading up to the house with its unguarded and fatally dangerous edges and corners restored discontent. When he parked the car and stepped out on to the ground, he was thoroughly gloomy.

Parra came out of the house, hurried to the car and opened the driving door. 'Good evening, Inspector. Nice to see you again.'

Did one have to be rich, Alvarez wondered, to accept servile politeness with pleasure? He went to close the door but was forestalled.

'I trust you are in good health, Inspector?'

'I'm still living.'

'Always welcome knowledge. The señorita noticed you drive in and said she expects you want to speak to her again. Perhaps you would like to come in now?'

'Later.'

'She will be glad to see you.'

'Perhaps.'

'She is very distressed.'

'Hardly surprising.'

'Is there any way in which I can help you?'

'No.'

'Please tell me if there should be.'

Alvarez was aware he had been rudely curt, but could not overcome his scorn for a Mallorquin who was so very polite because his job might depend on his being so.

He walked slowly towards the 'bow' of Barca. Already, he could feel the prickles which foretold the sweat of fear. Why continue? Why not confess to Salas he was unable to examine the rock around the orchid; could not, even if he were promised promotion to comisario. His rate of walking became still slower. Confession would be useless. Salas was too self-centred, too dismissive of others' failings to try to understand that mental strength could never overcome such terror.

As he came to a stop, he remembered Machado's last

words before the bands of the garrotte were drawn about his hooded head and neck. The weak die repeatedly before their deaths, the strong only when it arrives. He must be strong.

'Looking for something?'

Santos' words jerked his mind back to reality. The wooden barrier was only three metres away. He began to sweat.

'You look like you're about to pass out.'

Could words have been more inappropriate? 'Just thinking,' he croaked.

'Something wrong with your voice?'

'Sore throat.'

'Lemon and honey will soon see an end to that.'

'I'll try it as soon as I get home . . . Would you do something for me?'

'What prevents you from doing it yourself?'

'My leg's bad.'

'Seems like you're physically deteriorating very fast.'

'It sometimes gives way without warning and leaves me pretty-well immobilized.'

'Best carry a crutch around.'

'I'd be very grateful if you'd look to see if there's any sign of rock having fallen away recently from there.' He pointed.

'Is that where the señor went over?'

'Can't be certain, so it needs to be checked. I'd look for myself if it weren't for this damned leg.'

Santos whistled a few bars of unrecognizable music. 'It'd be best for you to do that in case I get things wrong, not being my job.'

'I trust your judgement as I would my own.'

'It's not the height that's worrying you?'

'No.'

'Then the thing for you to do, with that bad leg, is to get down on the ground and move forward until you can look over the edge. If I hang on to your legs, you'll be as safe as a man can be.'

'I can't climb over the fence.'

'Wriggle under the lower bar. Or maybe it don't look

right for an inspector to be seen crawling? All right, I'll do as you say and one day you can do me a good turn.'

Alvarez watched Santos climb the fence and walk to the edge of the rock with such assurance that the drop might have been only centimetres. Santos knelt and peered more closely at the rock face.

He returned to where Alvarez stood. 'There's been no breakaway – all the rock's weathered. There's a couple of marks which have recently scarred the weathering.'

'What would you reckon caused them?'

'Can't say.'

'The toes of shoes?'

Santos shrugged his shoulders.

'Thanks for your help.'

'Might be an idea to ask a doctor if your sore throat and wobbly leg are the result of nerves.'

There had been no need for sarcasm. Alvarez walked across to the house.

Parra opened the front door. 'Please come in, inspector.'

Mary was in the sitting room and was surprised to see him. It seemed Parra had not, as claimed, told her of his presence. Words spoken to make him feel more welcome than he was?

She returned his greeting and said: 'Still more questions?'

'I had to return here to check something and I hoped you wouldn't mind if I came in to ask how you were.'

'You think I might mind you were kind enough to care?' After a moment, she said: 'There's something I have to ask. When can I . . . can I arrange the funeral?'

'I fear I cannot say yet, señorita. You see . . .' He stopped.

'Well?'

'Because of what happened, there will have to be a post-mortem.'

She closed her eyes and gripped the arms of the chair.

Only a peaceful life admitted a peaceful death and then very rarely.

'It's the thought . . .' She moved her hands off the arms of the chair and joined them together in her lap. 'I want to apologize.'

'For what?' he asked in surprise.

'The way I behaved, embarrassing you last time.'

'I once knew too much sorrow ever to be embarrassed by another's sorrow. If you thought me that, it was because of my inability to help you.'

'You think you did not?'

'Then I am glad, señorita.'

'Please call me Mary. What is your name?'

'Enrique.'

'That's Henry in English, isn't it? A long, long time ago, I knew a boy called Henry. He made me a daisy chain and said it was . . . Oh, God! Talk to me about cabbages and kings, anything to stop me thinking about the past.'

'When my memory provides black times, I drive down to the bay. Quickly, or slowly, its beauty restores light. Come down to the bay and we will sit at one of the front cafés so that the magic works for you.'

'You want to drive me down and take me to a café? Out of pity?'

'Out of hope.'

'If you're lying, Enrique, it's a wonderful lie.'

SIX

Alvarez had left Mary at Aquila and was halfway down the descent from Barca when he realized he had forgotten something important and momentarily lost concentration on his driving. The car veered towards a drop of thirty metres. Instinct, rather than decisive thought, caused him to correct the mistake in time. He slowed to a crawl for the final drive down to the flat land.

It took time to recover from so close a brush with death. He parked near the old square, walked past tourists who had nothing to do but laze and drink, who did not risk their lives in the course of duty, and went into the bar at Club Llueso.

'Are you all right?' Roca asked as he put a brandy and a café cortado in front of Alvarez. 'You don't look your usual unhappy self.'

'I nearly had a fatal accident.'

'Happens all the time with foreigners on the wrong side of the road. Only last night I was retuning home . . .'

'I was half a centimetre from going over the edge.'

'If you had gone over, maybe you wouldn't have interrupted me when I was talking.'

'When you come as near to death as I did . . .'

'There's some who'd say you should have gone a little further.'

Alvarez carried brandy and coffee over to a newly vacated window table and sat. He drank most of the brandy and poured what remained into the coffee. Had he died, Roca would have been equally indifferent. Interested only in himself.

A young woman, who had been seated on her own at the next table, stood to leave. Had he been asked to criticize her, he would have had to remain silent. As she walked towards the door, a young man approached and it seemed he was introducing himself. Moments later, they left together. Alvarez watched them walk down the steps from the square to the road and knew bitter sorrow. Youth had deserted him and life offered no substitute. Had he approached her and suggested she might like to join him for dinner on his yacht, she would have welcomed the invitation; without a yacht, she would see him as a not-very-young, local yokel. He signalled to Roca he wanted another brandy.

'You're working very late,' Jaime said.

'What's that?' Alvarez was unable to hear clearly because the television, watched by Juan and Isabel, was presenting a pop group and the sound had been turned high.

Jaime shouted at the children to cut the row. Juan turned down the volume as little as he dared.

Dolores walked through the bead curtain. 'What is the trouble?'

'I was telling Juan to turn the sound down. Enrique and I couldn't hear each other.'

'That could be considered an advantage.'

Alvarez opened a door of the sideboard.

'You are thinking of having a drink now?' she asked.

'I need one.' He put glasses and a bottle on the table, poured himself a generous measure of Soberano and added ice. 'I've had a hell of a day.'

'You're always moaning about that,' Jaime commented.

'Because I am always suffering it.'

'What was the trouble this time? The boss wanted to know what work you've done over the past seven days?'

'You keep saying that.'

'You both appear to have very limited conversational powers,' Dolores observed, before she returned to the kitchen.

Alvarez drank. 'I had to spend much of the morning with the niece whose uncle fell over Barca. She's in a very emotional state. When I had to tell her there would be a post-mortem . . .' He swore at some length.

There was a swish of the bead curtain as Dolores returned. 'I have had to become used to my husband speaking words which no decent person should know, but it now seems my two innocent children are to learn others that are equally offensive from my cousin.'

'We've heard them on the box,' Juan said.

'Words spoken on that are often not permissible in a decent home.'

'But if Xelo says them . . .'

'His crudity will ensure your mouth is washed out with soap and water if ever I hear you speak them. And turn that noise down.'

'It's the latest number one . . .'

'You did not hear me?'

Juan turned the volume down again, and Dolores returned to the kitchen.

'Trust you,' Jaime muttered. 'Like as not, supper will be spoiled because you've upset her.'

'I swore because I suddenly remembered what I'd forgotten to remember.'

'You're sounding plain daft!'

Alvarez drank. Had he not been so upset by Mary's distress, he would not have thought to take her to the bay and he would have remembered the post-mortem; had he not fenced with death on his drive down from Barca, he would have recalled the time it was held . . . Miguel Vich had written that help given from a sense of self-congratulation was like a boomerang – it returned to strike one.

Sunday. A day of rest except for those unfortunate enough to serve under a man who held that all days were for work.

He phoned the morgue, identified himself and immediately began to explain why it had been impossible for him to have attended as he had intended . . .

'Why tell me? I'm just the attendant getting everything ready.'

'Is there anyone who can tell me the result of yesterday's PM.?'

'There wasn't one.'

'Why not?'

'It was cancelled.'

'Are you talking about Señor Gill?'

'If that's the Englishman who landed on his head. Going to be a job and a half to get him even halfway back to shape for the viewing.'

'His PM was scheduled for yesterday afternoon.'

'Doctor Jurando had an emergency – as you say, you did – and couldn't judge how long it would hold him, so said to delay until tomorrow morning.'

'At what time?'

'Midday.'

Miguel Vich had been wrong. The boomerang might return, but it could miss. He thanked the attendant, said he'd be at the morgue on Monday – *Why tell me? I'm just the attendant* – and replaced the receiver. The phone rang. Such was his sense of relief, he answered it immediately.

'The superior chief will speak to you,' Angela Torres said.

'Alvarez, I phoned you three times yesterday afternoon and three times there was no answer.'

'I was out, señor.'

'You find it necessary to underline the obvious? Or is it to cover the fact you could not be bothered to answer the calls?'

'I am surprised, señor, you should think I could ever behave in such a manner.'

'Then you are easily surprised. What has been learned from the post-mortem?'

'Nothing, because . . .'

'Because you forgot to attend.'

'It did not take place. Doctor Jurando was unable to conduct it yesterday. It will now be on Monday.'

'Why is there this delay?'

'Today is Sunday.'

'And you would agree that is a valid reason for not doing one's job? Why did you not inform me of the delay immediately you became aware of it?'

'There seemed little point in reporting a negative.'

'Your reports are frequently of that value. Have you conducted any further investigation into the death of the Englishman?'

'Of course, señor.'

'An optimistic assurance.'

'I returned to Barca and examined the edge of the rock face . . .'

'Why?'

'When I suggested perhaps a wedge of rock had given way when Señor Gill was standing on it, you ordered me to find out if that was so. Despite the height and sheer, dangerous drop, I examined the face. Nothing had recently broken away. But because the rock is well weathered, it was possible to distinguish two downward scrapes caused by the dead man as he fell.'

'If there has been no post-mortem, what is your authority for saying he suffered a stroke or cerebral bleed?'

'I don't understand.'

'I spoke very simply in order you should be able to do so.'

'I never suggested he had had a stroke or whatever the other thing is.'

'You named him as dead before he had completed the fall.'

'I was identifying him as the victim, señor, not suggesting he was dead as he fell.'

'An example of your inability to express your thoughts intelligibly. I presume you have not thought to ask at what time the PM is to take place.'

'Nine in the morning.'

'You will be there?'

'Of . . . Yes, señor.'

'You will inform me of the findings as soon as they are known. And refrain from giving the impression that the deceased was alive during the PM.'

The house in Carrer Julia Gayarre was little different in appearance from those around it, but some who passed it crossed themselves as they did and the more troublesome boys repeatedly tried to find a way of looking through the heavily glazed windows. Alvarez would have given much to be able to stare through them at the normal world beyond.

The post-mortem came to an end. Doctor Jurando

completed recording his findings, the overhead pod of lights was switched off, and the assistant began to clean and sterilize the instruments before 'tidying up' the body.

Jurando removed gown and surgeon's gloves, dropped them into a disposal bag. He spoke to Alvarez. 'I'm sorry about the delay, but I had to deal with a very serious emergency yesterday.'

'There was no problem. In fact –' Alvarez hastily changed what he had been about to say – 'it enabled me to complete some work.'

'Death was due to crushing injuries to the head and would have been instantaneous. Two small pieces of rock were embedded in the fractured skull.'

'The fall definitely killed him?'

'Yes.'

'So it's straightforward?' Alvarez managed to conceal his relief.

'The cause of death, yes. But the cause of the fall . . . That is your problem.'

'Surely he must have misjudged his footing or tripped and went over the edge?'

'There are inconsistencies.'

There would be, Alvarez thought bitterly. Foreigners seemed unable to die in an uncomplicated manner.

'There is recent bruising to the stomach. One would expect that; during his fall, it was likely he would have struck the rock.'

'Then I don't quite see the problem?'

'He was wearing a cotton T-shirt and shorts. On the shirt and top of the shorts, corresponding to the position of the bruising, there are no signs of contact – no scuffed or torn material, no rock stains.'

'Contact must have been very brief.'

'Yet of sufficient force to cause the considerable bruising. In the circumstances, would you not have expected the clothing to have suffered?'

Alvarez tried to find circumstances in which he would not and failed.

'There were further injuries of an internal nature. These

are consistent with the victim having suffered blows of considerable force.'

'Caused when he struck the rock face?'

'I doubt it.'

Alvarez knew irritated despair. Problems meant careful enquiries, enquiries meant endless work.

'How did the shirt lie on him when he was on the ground?'

'It was slightly disarranged, but it was down over his chest.'

'Probably held down by the rush of wind, since he was falling head first.'

'Are you saying he was attacked?'

'It seems probable.'

Alvarez phoned Palma.

Angela Torres answered, her voice more plum-laden than ever. 'The superior chief is not in his office.'

'Enjoying an early siesta?' Alvarez asked.

'You consider that amusing?'

'I'll try again around five.'

'You will be returning from lunch early?' she asked sweetly.

'Ah, yes!' Salas said. 'The inspector who suggested I wasted my time with a siesta.'

Even if she *was* a woman, Alvarez thought, Angela Torres might have kept silent. 'There was no intention to criticize, señor.'

'Yet you insolently succeeded.'

'I attended the post-mortem of Señor Gill.'

'The result?'

'The cause of death was the injuries to his head. Death would have been immediate, so he was fortunate.'

'You do not find it to be lacking in moral decency to refer to a premature and violent death as fortunate?'

'I was meaning the probability he could not have fully understood what was about to happen. When something catastrophic occurs, shock may briefly still the brain and black out conscious knowledge.'

'You are an expert on the brain?'

'No, but—'

'That is all there is to report?'

'No, señor. In addition to the injuries to the head, there was bruising to the stomach, yet there was no damage to the material of shirt or shorts, no evidence of contact with the rock.'

'A man can fall in an arc.'

'There was also heavy bruising to the stomach and internal injuries consistent with heavy blows.'

'If I have managed to understand you, Señor Gill might have been assaulted before he fell?'

'That is what Doctor Jurando said.'

'You are now telling me this may be a case of murder?'

'It seems so.'

'Then the only possibility you have not so far suggested is natural causes.'

'My investigation will soon resolve the nature of the death.'

'I have never received evidence to confirm your optimism.'

'If it was suicide, there would surely have been evidence of a distracted mind. The staff have told me there was no such suggestion. I will question the señorita to learn her impression of her uncle's mental state.'

'Yet no doubt not before you are satisfied that by doing so you will not distress her further?'

'Something one has to remember is that the señor was wealthy.'

'Did you not inform me he was worried about money?'

'I don't think the suggestion was that he had become hard up. In rough times, people often try to appear short of money in order to avoid the envy of the less fortunate.'

'You are wealthy?'

'Far from it.'

'Then you are again indulging yourself by asserting facts about which you can know nothing.'

'It makes common sense.'

'Then you are even less qualified to comment.'

'Señor, where there is money, there is anticipation. Amongst those who benefit from the señor's death, there may well have been one prepared to commit murder in order to do so.'

'You will search for a motive in order to judge if this case is one of murder?'

'Motive makes murder. And there is possible motive in that the señor had a friend. A very close friend.'

'I fail to see the significance of that.'

'She was married.'

'You are suggesting an illicit relationship because you are unable to understand that a man and a woman can enjoy a platonic friendship?'

'In this case, there is evidence it was not platonic. Which means the husband may have known of his wife's adultery and taken his revenge.'

'Then you will question the husband.'

'I think I will question the wife on her own, first.'

'Why?'

'If she confesses her adultery, and can assure me her husband has no knowledge of it, it will eliminate him as a suspect.'

'You do not consider it your duty to inform him of her infidelity?'

'Certainly not my duty, nor even a moral obligation. Since Señor Gill is dead, the affair cannot continue. So where is the point of bringing pain to the marriage?'

'Your attitude is deplorable.'

'I would call it realistic.'

'To condone adultery displays depravity, not realism.'

'I don't agree.'

'I have not asked for your opinion. What else do you have to report?'

'A very strong motive, judged by the present evidence. The señor had a bitter row with a local who was in his wood and whom he suspected was after birds. The feathered kind.'

'You know of birds without feathers?'

'It is an expression in common use.'

'What does it mean?'

'Young ladies.'

'You introduce the subject for no reason other than your depravity?'

'Santos, who is the gardener at Aquila—'

'There is no need constantly to waste time by telling me something of which I am well aware.'

'He heard the señor, who was below Barca, having a very acrimonious row with a man. The señor accused the man, in Spanish, of poaching thrushes and being a thief. Threatened to bring in the policia local.'

'You are claiming the poacher had a motive for the señor's murder?'

'Yes.'

'That does not strike you as somewhat absurd – a man murders because he is accused of poaching and is called a thief?'

'When a Mallorquin is addressed in such terms, especially when correctly, he may develop a sudden, unthinking anger, which can turn to violence. It's said to be a trait inherited from Moorish ancestors.'

'A nonsensical excuse for an unforgivable temper. Have you questioned this man?'

'No.'

'Why not?'

'I don't know who he was.'

'And see this as an excuse for not taking steps to find out?'

'Santos can give me no hint of his identity since he never saw him and didn't recognize his voice.'

'You will not have considered that Santos may well be aware of who it was? You will identify and question this poacher.'

'But if—'

'But and if are words which have no place in the cuerpo.'

'Yet how does one—'

'By carrying out the order.' Salas replaced his receiver.

SEVEN

Alvarez remained behind the wheel until he had overcome emotions aroused by the drive up to Aquila. He finally stepped out of the car, crossed to the front door and rang the bell.

The door was opened by a young woman, just short of twenty, who remained slim, as modern Mallorquin women were tending to do. Her face was round; hair, deep black; eyes, dark brown; nose, snub. Although not a close lookalike, she did remind him of . . . He couldn't remember the name, only the passion. 'I'm Inspector Alvarez. And you are Eva?'

'How d'you know that?' The question had disturbed her.

'I was told you worked here and haven't met you before.'

'I thought . . .'

He wondered what she had thought? 'Shall I come in?'

She became flustered. 'I should have said.'

He stepped into the hall. 'Is Parra not here?'

'Him and Luisa have gone into Inca.'

'And the señorita?'

'She's in the sitting room, watching television. Doesn't do much else.'

She had spoken with little feeling. One had to approach middle age and understand the fears of one's future to sympathize with the burdens of others.

She made no move to show him into the sitting room. He preferred her indifference to the finer points of staff service to Parra's over-indulgence in them. As he entered, Mary looked away from the television set and at him. 'I hope you don't mind my turning up without warning?'

She used the remote to switch off the television. 'Of course not. You're looking rather stern.'

'I have to tell you something.'

'Which is going to be horrid.' She looked away.

He sat. 'Your uncle may not have died accidentally.'

'Then what happened?'

'Might he have been sufficiently worried and depressed to commit suicide?'

'Never! It's a horrible suggestion.'

'He was rather depressed.'

'Was he?'

'So I've been told.'

'By whom?'

'I can't remember. Perhaps there were many worries with the present financial chaos . . .'

'He said we'd be more careful because no one knew how the markets would move, but we'd no need to worry.'

'He could have wanted not to disturb you.'

'Don't you understand? He wouldn't have killed himself whatever happened. He thought it the coward's way out.'

'You seem very certain.'

'I am.'

Would Gill have told her the true situation?

'Have you any more ridiculous, horrible suggestions?'

He longed to say 'no'. 'I'm afraid that if he could never have committed suicide, it's possible he was deliberately killed.'

Her face expressed shock. 'Christ!' Her voice rose. 'Isn't it cruel enough that he's dead? Now you come and say someone may have hated him so much, he was murdered. How could anyone hate so horribly?'

'If it is the truth, I will find out.'

'Why don't you know the truth?'

'If I were clever, perhaps I would.'

'I . . . Please, take me down to the bay again.'

They were seated at a table set out on the sand, a straw south-sea sun cover providing shade. In front of her was an as yet untouched glass of Maquis Murietta rosado, in front of him an empty glass. He checked the time. 'I'm afraid we should move if you have an early lunch.'

'Normally, it's at one,' she answered.

'For us, that is early.'

'I'm not hungry.'

He was. 'Will your meal be waiting for you?'

'No. I said I didn't know what I wanted and would tell them when I decided.'

'Shall I ring your home and ask them to prepare what-ever you choose?'

'Luisa is away with Pablo; Eva hasn't learned to cook.'

'That's unusual.' To talk might briefly blanket memories and fears. 'But probably not so much these days. Cooking is a skill, good cooking, a skill presented by the gods. The young no longer are prepared to take the trouble to learn the art; they do not understand a happy marriage comes with a contented husband. Why bother to cook when one can go into a shop and buy something frozen which merely has to be put into a microwave? That it tastes of nothing does not worry them.'

'Luisa is a good cook.'

'A pity you did not suggest what you might like so that she could prepare it.'

'She and Pablo are away this morning,' she repeated.

'Of course.'

She drank briefly. 'Do you like Chinese food?'

'I don't know.'

'You mean, you've never eaten it?'

She was not as depressed as she had been when they arrived. The magic of the bay was working once again. 'I live with my cousin and she regards with uneasiness all foods which aren't traditional to the island or the Peninsula.'

'Then you have the chance to find out if you do or don't like it. Have a takeaway lunch with me.'

'Today?'

'You sound alarmed.'

He was. Recently there had been a programme on television which had shown people eating in a Shanghai restaurant. Live snakes had been brought to the table, the host had chosen which he wanted, and it had been decapi-tated, skinned and cooked. What else might there be in a Chinese meal? Rats, puppy dogs' tails . . . ? 'Lunch with

you would be very pleasant, but unfortunately I have to
return to the office quite soon. Perhaps some other day?'

'I'll hold you to that.'

Alvarez called a waiter and paid the bill. They walked
across the sand to the roadway and his parked car.

He opened the front passenger door as, so he had been
told, did an English gentleman.

'Are you sure you have the time to take me home?' she
asked.

He smiled. 'Are you prepared to walk?'

'I can get a taxi.'

'Not when I'm here to drive you.'

He braked to a halt in front of Aquila.

'Thank you for everything, Enrique.'

'It has been nothing.'

'Don't be silly. But for you, I'd still be sitting and looking
at the television and not knowing what was showing . . .
Enrique?'

'Yes?'

She hesitated. 'Just friends.' She hurried into the house.

Alvarez sat at the table and poured himself a reviving brandy.
'D'you reckon lunch is about ready?'

'She's not here,' Jaime answered.

'How d'you mean?'

'Cooking a meal for some old biddy who can't do it for
herself.'

'What about us?'

'That's what I asked. Got my head bitten off, told I didn't
know the meaning of being charitable.'

'It shouldn't mean having to starve.'

'Not exactly starve. She's left something warming in the
oven for us.'

'You could have said.' He poured a good measure of
Soberano. 'It's all very well leaving the food warm, but it
won't be as good as if it had just been cooked.'

'You think I don't know that?'

'Not like her to expect us to eat a poor meal.'

'Tell her so yourself.'

'You're in a sharp mood.'

'Got reason, haven't I? Ignoring what I want.'

'Wives never worry about that.'

'How would you know?'

'Seen it happen often enough.'

'Well, it doesn't happen in this house.'

Alvarez wondered if Jaime, considering what went on his house, was joking. It seemed he was not. 'It's been an annoying morning,' Alvarez said.

'Never anything else for you.'

'I've been asked to identify a man who no one's seen.'

'So he's invisible.'

'Santos – he's the gardener at Aquila—'

'Think I don't know that?'

'Trying to sound like the superior chief? Santos was up on Barca and heard a fierce row going on below. One bloke was the señor, the other a Mallorquin. I've been ordered to identify him. Since Santos never saw him and couldn't tell who it was from the voice, how the hell am I supposed to do that?'

'Wouldn't know.'

'According to Santos, the argument was about birds. The señor had said that someone was after them on his land, and it seems likely that's who he was cursing for poaching. But how am I supposed to find out who was after the thrushes?'

'Thrushes?'

'That's right.'

'How d'you know that?'

'I don't, but that's what the señor said to Santos. I suppose the señor saw a net or maybe a load of feathers.'

'So how would he know they came from thrushes?'

'There are a lot of people who can tell the make of a bird from its feathers.'

'Not difficult if it's a peacock. Catching thrushes is illegal these days.'

'Quite.'

'I like 'em. Can't understand why they were made illegal. No one says you can't catch sparrows.'

'Ever heard of anyone wanting to eat one?'

'No.'

'Then it'll be because they taste lousy.' Alvarez drank. 'How can I be expected to identify an unknown man with no description, nothing to single him out from a thousand and one other men?'

Jaime spoke reminiscently. 'Thrushes weren't in danger of becoming extinct. It was the EU made 'em illegal. I'd make the EU illegal. I bought three thrushes a while back. Cost the earth. Brought 'em back and said she could cook 'em for supper. You know what? I had to wait until you was out for supper, and so they weren't real fresh.'

'Why did I have to be away?'

'Since they were illegal, you couldn't eat one.'

'I'd have said it was a delicious partridge.'

'You can't keep quiet and would have said as how you hadn't enjoyed thrush for a long time. You'd know I'd broken the law and might have reported me.'

'She said that?'

'Yes.'

'Women can't think straight.' Alvarez had enjoyed thrushes when they could appear on the menu. He sadly remembered how Dolores had cooked them to perfection and made a memorable sauce to go with them. He could almost conjure up the exquisite taste in his mouth, but since he couldn't succeed, he suffered frustration. How could she have let them forgo the pleasure of such a meal in the stupid belief he would report anyone? Irritated incomprehension then gave way to curiosity. 'You bought them? From whom?'

'Why d'you want to know?'

'Because he might be the man who was netting in Barca and had a furious row with Señor Gill.'

'What if it was?'

'He might be able to help me.'

'You think he'd want to?'

'I won't be arresting him or anything stupid like that. I just want to know who it was so I can ask him about the señor. I'd make it clear all I sought was information.'

'Can't remember who it was.'

'Try harder.'

Jaime drained his glass. 'I'm telling you, I can't remember.'

'You're a poor liar.'

'You think I'm going to rat on him?'

'I've explained . . .'

'Didn't hear.'

'Becoming deaf as you grow older?'

'That's right.'

'But not disinterested.'

'How d'you mean?'

'I saw you in the square a week ago.'

'What if you did?'

'You were having a friendly chat with someone.'

'If you mean . . . I was at school with her. We just met by chance and were chatting about the old days.'

'And the old days were fun for her and you? I suppose you mentioned meeting her to Dolores?'

Jaime didn't answer.

'I suppose that, even if it was just good friendship, it's better if she doesn't know and get the wrong idea. By the way, have you remembered the name of the seller of the thrushes?'

'Are you saying that if I don't tell you . . .' Jaime's sense of outrage became so great that he could not finish the sentence.

Alvarez shrugged his shoulders.

Jaime refilled his glass. 'Now I know why Santiago said you could be a real bastard.' He drank, put the glass down on the table. 'Lorenzo Velaquez. And I hope he tells you to go to hell!'

Isabel, followed by Juan, hurried into the room. She went to switch on the television.

'Let it be,' Jaime said.

'It's my favourite programme,' she protested.

'They all are.'

Juan switched on the television.

'Didn't you hear?' Jaime demanded.

'It was her you told, not me.'

'Trying to be a smart little—' He stopped abruptly as Dolores came in from the entrada.

She faced him. 'What were you about to call our son?'

'Nothing.'

'You think him to be nothing? I bore nothing, nurtured nothing, have to defend nothing from a father who can think only of himself?'

'You don't understand.'

'My misfortune is that I do.' She stared at the table. 'You have both eaten?'

'Not yet.'

'Because you have not finished drinking?' She went through to the kitchen, soon reappeared. 'The meal is ready. Since you have already drunk too much to judge what you eat, it is Albóndigas de patata y carne.' She returned to the kitchen.

'Why won't she understand?' Jaime moaned.

And why can't you realize, Alvarez thought, that a wise man never argues with a woman, he lets her go on talking nonsense.

There was a call from the kitchen. 'You can come through and collect things.'

No one moved.

She came out of the kitchen, a filled plate, knife and fork in her hands. She sat at the table.

'What about us?' Jaime asked.

'You will eventually decide whether or not to eat.'

'But . . . You always put everything on the table.'

'That I have not done so now proves you wrong.'

Alvarez reluctantly went into the kitchen. She had not even put out plates and cutlery for them. Something very serious had disturbed her. Jaime's unspoken description of Juan seemed too insignificant to warrant going on strike.

He carried his plate to the dining table, refilled his glass with wine and ate. The meatballs were admittedly tasty, but they would surely have been tastier had she taken the trouble to cook them and serve them immediately.

Dolores addressed Juan and Isabel. 'Like your father, you consider me to be the maid?'

Unlike their father, they had learned to read the danger signs. They hastily went into the kitchen.

'I met Julia in the village,' she said when she had finished her meal.

'Because you couldn't disappear quickly enough?' Jaime suggested.

'You are careless that she is a friend?'

'The last time you mentioned her, you called her a stupid cow.'

'I never descend, as do you, to the language of the gutter.'

Juan and Isabel returned with their meals.

Dolores spoke to Alvarez. 'She mentioned she saw you earlier today.'

'Fortunately, I didn't see her.'

'She asked if you'd lost your job.'

'As rudely curious as ever.'

'She could not understand why you were sitting at one of the tables on the beach when you should have been working.'

'I was.'

'Then it was not you who was drinking with a young woman with auburn hair and an unfortunate injury to her face?'

Jaime smiled broadly, happy to see Alvarez suffer as he had done.

Juan said, 'Was she one of uncle's . . . What does daddy call them? Buns?'

'It is time for you and Isabel to go up for an afternoon's rest,' Dolores said.

'I remember now.'

'You did not hear me?'

Juan stood. 'One of uncle's tarts.'

'You are making me very angry.'

Juan, followed by Isabel, hurried upstairs.

Jaime said: 'Now I know why Enrique was working on the beach. She was very difficult to persuade.'

'You find it necessary to expose your crudity?' Dolores asked.

'That was being amusing.'

'As my mother used to say, a man finds his amusement where a lady will not tread.' She turned to Alvarez. 'This woman is a foreigner?'

'English.'

'Younger than you?'

'By several years.'

'It appeals to your vanity that she should drink with you?'

'I wouldn't say that.'

'You can think she sees you not as you are, but as you would like to be; she will not notice your hair is thinning . . .'

'It is not.'

'. . . that your skin is creased and your belly swells. You lie and believe yourself to be irresistible.'

'I believe I am irreplaceable.'

'Even my dear mother would not have thought a man could be so mistaken.'

'The young lady was the person I have mentioned before whose uncle has just died.'

'That is the truth?'

'The unvarnished truth.'

'Julia was trying to make fun of me?'

'It would seem like it.'

'She is a cow.'

'Didn't you go for me a moment ago because . . .' Jaime stopped as she glared at him.

'I might briefly seem irreplaceable to her,' Alvarez continued, 'because when she is overtaken with bitter sorrow, I help her a little when I take her down to the bay. And to make the situation perfectly clear, the final thing she said to me was "Just friends".'

'Warning you off,' Jaime said. 'Now she must be rich, she reckons you could be thinking of doing some good for yourself.'

'Can there be another man as insensitive as you?' she asked.

'Why say that?'

'Because you cannot understand the reason she spoke as

she did was she did not want Enrique to be embarrassed by the thought that she might be beginning to regard him with affection.'

'How d'you know it's not the other way round?'

'Aiyee! If women could look into the future, there would be very few marriages.'

EIGHT

Dolores' call finally awoke Alvarez. He looked at his watch and was vaguely surprised to learn he was already half an hour late for his return to work. He would get up immediately, forgo coffee, and hurry to the office.

'I had to call you several times,' Dolores said as he entered the kitchen fifteen minutes later.

He was surprised she spoke without any hint of criticism. 'I was so fast asleep, I didn't hear you until the last call. I suppose that's because it was such an emotionally exhausting morning.'

'I will make your coffee.'

'I think I'll have to leave that and rush to the office . . .'

'You will drink coffee and eat a biscuit or two. A man needs a happy stomach before he works.'

'You sometimes say mine is too happy.'

'What nonsense is that? A man who does not eat well insults the cook. Sit down while I make coffee and bring some of those chocolate biscuits you like so much.'

He pulled a chair from under the table and sat. He'd no idea why she was in so generous a mood, could only hope it would last.

She placed a plate of chocolate digestives on the table, crossed to a working surface and prepared the coffee machine. 'I phoned Julia earlier.'

To find out if his companion on the beach had been a blonde in a monokini?

'I told her she had been very wrong. That annoyed her for a start. She cannot believe she is ever wrong.' She switched on the coffee machine, went over to the refrigerator for a plastic carton of milk, then to one of the cupboards for a dish of sugar and placed everything in front of him. 'Is there anything more you would like?'

'No, thanks.'

She absent-mindedly picked up a biscuit and ate. 'I said it was unfortunate she believed you had been entertaining when you were so kindly helping a niece who had just lost her uncle. I added how sad it was that some people cannot stop jumping to nasty conclusions because their minds live in shadows.' The coffee machine hissed. She turned it off, poured coffee into a mug, carried this over to the table. 'Was I not right to criticize her?'

'Absolutely.'

'She will not phone me again in order to speak poisonous nonsense.'

He added milk to the coffee. Were he a brave man, he would have reminded her of how often she jumped to wrong conclusions, but there were times when a sensible man was a coward.

The phone rang as Alvarez stepped into the office. He needed to sit down and recover his breath, but instinct said the caller was Salas. He lifted the receiver as he stood at the side of the desk. 'Inspector Alvarez speaking.'

'What have you to report?' Salas asked.

'I am making enquiries, señor.'

'That is not what I asked.'

'I have spoken to Señorita Farren at length. She is convinced her uncle would never have committed suicide.'

'Her grounds for that?'

'I did not press her because she was in so distressed a state. In addition, I was going to have to explain that there was the possibility her uncle had been murdered.'

'As so often, you judged it would be best to do nothing.'

'There are benefits from taking an investigation slowly, señor.'

'A proposition to which you hold firmly. How wealthy was Señor Gill at the time of his death?'

'I haven't yet been able to find out.'

'Because of the fact that motive can identify murder and the murderer has escaped you?'

'I have said as much to you, señor.'

'No doubt, incoherently. Put simply, if Señor Gill remained

rich at the time of his death – despite the heavy losses others have sustained – there is motive for his murder. Who will inherit his estate?'

'I don't yet know.'

'The importance of knowing has also escaped you?'

'I am intending to return to Aquila to speak to Señorita Farren again. I will ask her about the details of her uncle's will, if she knows them.'

'It will be of little use to ask, if she doesn't. Whom do you expect to be the main beneficiary?'

'She is the obvious person, but the señor might well have other relatives and friends about whom we know nothing; one or more of them may inherit.'

'Do you understand the importance of what you have just said?'

'I . . . With particular reference to what?'

'Rule out suicide and accident and the niece becomes the prime suspect for his murder.'

'That's ridiculous!'

Salas spoke sharply. 'I do not expect an inspector to address me in such terms.'

'But she is incapable of such a crime. She was extremely fond of him. He was the one person who provided the protection she needed. If you'd seen her distress when I asked her if she thought her uncle might have committed suicide . . . Her tears!'

'Women use tears as a smokescreen.'

'I am certain she could have had no part in his death.'

'You wish to deny motive is the key and money provides the strongest of motives?'

'That's true, but . . .'

'You find difficulty in acknowledging truth.'

'Señor, there is a motive as strong, or even stronger, than money. The jealousy of a betrayed husband.'

'When you enjoyed informing me about the adultery, you said you would question the wife when her husband was not present so that he should not learn about her promiscuity. He will not have gained revenge for something of which he was ignorant.'

'There has to be the possibility he did know about it, but his wife did not know that he knew.'

'You can imagine he would accept such knowledge with equanimity?'

'Perhaps he gained an advantage from his wife's affair.'

'A sick possibility which could only occur to a sick mind. And in your eagerness, you overlook the fact the husband, if there can be one so perverse in character, would be unlikely to bring to an end a relationship which benefited him.'

'Suppose she had persuaded him that what they were receiving was only a fraction of what they could gain if she divorced him and Señor Gill wanted to marry her? She should continue the affair until marriage was offered. But her husband realized the truth – she was certain the offer of marriage would be given and since she would be divorced, she could marry Señor Gill, enjoy all his wealth, and forget her first husband. He was so outraged by her moral scheming and infidelity that he murdered the señor in revenge.'

There was a long silence.

'Are you there, señor?'

'I strongly doubt I have ever had to listen to someone to whom depravity comes so naturally.'

'It has to be best to consider all possibilities.'

'Not when proposed from a mind such as yours.'

'I think . . .'

'I do not wish to listen to any more of your obnoxious thoughts. When this call is ended, you will consider Señor Gill's niece as the prime suspect and question her concerning details of the señor's will and of his finances. Have you identified the poacher?'

'I may have done.'

'You have not questioned him to find out if for once you have succeeded in your job?'

'Señor, it will take a long time to do all you have asked.'

'When I was an inspector, I never expected to be in bed before midnight.'

The stone-built caseta had one bedroom, one main room which doubled as a kitchen, a primitive bathroom with no running water, and a long drop outside. Decades before, many lived in such confined quarters, now Velaquez, whose features displayed years spent working in sun, wind and rain, was one of a very few. He was in the field using a cut-down can to pour water into one of the irrigation channels drawn through the earth, on either side of which vegetables grew.

'They look nice,' Alvarez said, indicating a bunch of tomatoes beginning to turn red.

Velaquez emptied the tin into the channel, stood upright. He looked briefly at Alvarez, walked over to a well and manually pumped up water to fill the can. He returned, began to empty the can. 'You're Dolores Ramis' cousin.'

'That's right.'

'Interested in tomatoes?'

'When they have some taste . . . I've come to have a chat about Barca and the land around it.'

'Where?'

'Where you often like to walk.'

'Who says?'

'Everyone who knows you.'

'Ain't no harm in that.'

'Depends why you're there. Likely you find something special about the place?'

'It's quiet.'

'But not always peaceful?'

'Can't say.'

'Seems there was a violent row below Barca not so long ago.'

'Was there?'

'Señor Gill found someone there he reckoned was netting thrushes.'

'No one does that now it's illegal.'

'Doesn't make much difference to some people.'

Velaquez began to move away. 'Got to keep watering.'

'When I say. You knew Señor Gill died from a fall?'

'Yes.'

'It's possible someone pushed him over. Why should anyone want to do that?'

'Why ask me?'

'Thought you'd be able to give an answer.'

'Never met him.'

'Not when you strolled through the peaceful woods?'

'No.'

'He reckoned someone was after birds, and that infuriated him because he wanted them to have peace.'

'It ain't nothing to do with me.'

'Not if he reckoned you were netting thrushes.'

'Don't know what you're on about.'

'The row you had with the señor made you very, very angry.'

'I said, ain't never met him.'

'You aren't helping yourself by lying. Do you know Juanito Santos?'

'No.'

'Does the garden at Aquila. He heard the row and recognized the two voices. Señor Gill's and yours.'

'He's a liar.'

'Or it's a wrong vocal identification? I don't think so.'

'Don't matter what you think. It wasn't me. Never met the señor, and I ain't ever gone after thrushes.'

'Then where do you get the ones you sell?'

'Don't sell none.'

'I've heard from several villagers that they've bought thrushes from you, even though you charge a fortune.'

'They're lying.'

'Seems there's a lot of liars around. Look, I don't want to take you in, but go on like this and I'll have to.'

'Take me where?'

'To one of the cells at the post.'

'You can't prove nothing.'

'Then where do the thrushes you sell come from?'

'I don't sell any.'

'Then you will have to come along with me.'

'For catching thrushes when I ain't?'

'On suspicion of murdering Señor Gill.'

Velaquez suffered uncomprehending fear. 'You can't . . . I didn't . . . I've never . . .'

'If he was murdered, why? There's no one else with any reason to do so. He caught you in the woods and aggressively accused you of illegal trapping. Likely said he was calling the policia local. You've been in trouble before,' Alvarez guessed.

'Not for anything serious. Never been in jail.'

'Count yourself lucky. Only, your luck's kind of running out. Trapping thrushes gets all those love-life people very angry. For a bloke like you, living free, being stuck in a cell for months couldn't be worse. So to save yourself a living purgatory, tell me what did happen. You went up to Aquila—'

'I didn't.'

'Maybe you originally thought you'd just apologize and ask him to be generous and forget what happened. He was at the end of Barca, tending his orchid. He wouldn't listen to you, said he hoped you'd be jailed for years. In a desperate attempt to save yourself, you pushed him over the edge.'

'That's crazy. I've never been up there. You've got to believe me.'

'You lied about selling thrushes, didn't you?'

'That don't mean I killed him.'

'You now admit you trapped thrushes there?'

After a while, Velaquez muttered an admission.

'Then where were you at thirteen hundred hours on the fourth?'

'How would I know? Don't mean nothing to me what the time is, or the day.'

'That is when the señor fell to his death. And you had reason to wish him dead.'

'Kill a man just because . . . Here, wasn't that a Friday?'

'Days do suddenly mean something to you?'

'I was in hospital having me shoulder X-rayed.' Velaquez spoke with the breathless haste of someone seeking continued life when in sight of the gallows.

Alvarez phoned the hospital. As was to be expected, he had to flaunt the superior chief's name before he could persuade someone to check the records. Lorenzo Velaquez had had his shoulder X-rayed at thirteen hundred hours on the fourth.

*   *   *

The sun had set behind the mountains, but the light was still reasonably good; there was a mauve tinge to the northern sky. Above the mountains, a black vulture circled the spot where food was put out for the few remaining birds to keep them fit and encourage them to breed.

Alvarez left his car. Parra opened the front door as he neared it.

'You are becoming a frequent visitor, Inspector.'

'No need to be alarmed.'

Parra smiled. 'I am glad. Inspector, do you mind if I ask you something?'

'I won't know until you say what you want.'

'The señorita sadly has been very disturbed, so when she told me you think the señor may not have suffered an accident, he may have committed suicide or been murdered, I wondered if she had become very confused.'

'Murder is one possibility I am having to investigate.'

'It is very difficult to believe that possible.'

'Why?'

'He was a kind man.'

'Which left him more at risk.'

Mary was watching the television. She managed a brief smile of welcome. 'Come and sit down, Enrique.' She turned to Parra who was standing in the doorway. 'Yes, Pablo?'

'I thought you might like coffee or a drink, señorita.'

'I imagine the inspector would like a drink. If I remember correctly, it is coñac with just ice. And I'll have coffee.'

Parra left.

After Juana-María had died, he had experienced times of false acceptance. Would Mary find the return of sorrow as quick and as cruel as he had done?

'Are you here to ask more questions?' she asked.

'I'm afraid so.'

'Then let's get it over and done with as soon as possible.'

'Will you remind me of the name of the lady with whom your uncle was friendly.'

'Virginia Oakley.'

'Where does she live?'

'In Port Xalon.'

'Do you know her address?'

'You . . . Are you going to speak to her?'

'I have to talk to everyone who knew your uncle.'

'Paul can't have known about Robin and Virginia.'

'I need to make certain of that.'

'Must you?'

He did not answer.

'Paul will learn.'

'Only if it becomes absolutely essential he does.'

'You'll try to save her from all the beastly trouble there could be? You're not at all like a detective.'

'My superior chief would agree.'

'He is not an understanding man?'

'A very misunderstanding one.'

Parra returned, placed sugar, milk and cup of coffee on her table, and handed Alvarez a well-stocked glass. He left.

She added sugar and milk to the cup, drank, replaced the cup on its saucer. 'You want her address. Ca'n Alzenar. I can't tell you any more because I've never been there, but I do know it's not far back from the sea front.'

'Thank you.'

'Now can we talk about fun things.'

'I still have to ask . . .'

'I'm not going to answer any more questions. You'll have to come back again. Have you seen the latest blockbuster film? Moira saw it and said it scared her silly, but she always goes over the top. Do you like musicals? I don't know how many times I've watched *My Fair Lady* . . .'

He said little, merely encouraging her to continue telling him about fun things.

Port Xalon was on the south coast. Fifty years previously, there had been a small village inland, while on the sea front were huts in which the fishermen kept their gear and spent the nights before sailing off at daybreak. Eternal optimists, their hope was always for a catch which would sell for sufficient pesetas to enable them to return home to rest and buy their families wholesome and plentiful food. Now, it was a tourist centre which had escaped becoming a concrete jungle due to an enlightened council. In the marina, there were many boats, sail and power, which might go out to sea only a dozen times in a year; most had cost more than any fisherman had earned in several years.

Alvarez braked to a halt in front of the small bungalow in a two hundred square metre plot, at the end of a line of four similar houses. He climbed out of the car, locked it with the remote, opened ornamental wrought-iron gates, walked up the chipped-rock path, knocked on the front door. This was opened by a woman in her mid thirties, contemporarily slim, neatly dressed and made-up, but not a potential catwalk beauty.

'Señora Oakley?'

'Yes.'

'I am Inspector Alvarez of the Cuerpo General de Policia.'

'You're . . . a policeman?'

'That is so.'

'Has something happened to my husband; to Paul?'

'Nothing has happened to him, señora. I merely wish to ask you a few questions.'

'About what?'

'I will explain. Perhaps I might enter your house to escape the sun while we talk?'

'I . . . I suppose so.'

Entry was directly into a small sitting room, neatly but budget-furnished. On the far wall hung the painting of an island scene that was now seldom met – a tumble-down caseta, fronted by prickly pear cacti and an almond tree in blossom. Tumbledown fincas waiting to be reformed by foreigners were now as rare as traditional corner shops. She sat on the settee, he on a chair.

'I'm afraid, señora, I do have unwelcome news. However, I hasten to add it does not concern your husband.'

'Who then?'

'Señor Gill.'

She looked away. 'Who?'

'He had a serious fall which unfortunately proved to be fatal.'

She no longer tried to suggest the name was unfamiliar.

There was a brief moan; she brushed tears from her eyes
with her forefinger, then had to use a handkerchief. Her
shoulders shook, and she pressed her lips tightly together
to try to stop them trembling.

'I believe you were close friends.'

She shook her head.

'I need to learn as much about him as I can. You may
be able to help me.'

'We were just . . . just casual friends, Robin and me. I'm
sorry, but I have to go out so if you don't mind leaving?'

'I will not keep you for long if you can tell me whether
Señor Gill seemed in any way disturbed in the past few
weeks.'

'We've only seen him a couple of times in months.'

'Did he seem to be depressed?'

'No.'

'Did he mention any financial problems? That he had
had money in one of the failed banks?'

'Why do you want to know?'

'There has to be the possibility he committed suicide.'

'Never!' she said loudly and forcefully.

'You seem very certain.'

'I am.'

'Why?'

She hesitated. 'I can't say, but I know he would never
do that.'

'I understand he had friends in Andraitx.'

The sudden change in subject bemused her.

'Their name is Green. Your husband frequently spends a
day with them, but you seldom go with him. I should like
to know why that is?'

'I don't get on with Prue.'

'She is Señora Green?'

'Yes.'

'When your husband is with them, what do you do?'

'It could be anything. How can I answer?'

'By telling me the truth.'

'I don't see why I should say . . .' Distress had given way
to sharp concern.

'Perhaps you met Señor Gill here?'

She flinched. Her voice rose. 'What are you hinting at? You've no right to say such things.'

'I have that right, señora, you have the duty to answer my questions. Did Señor Gill visit here when your husband was in Andraitx.'

'Of course he didn't. It's a filthy suggestion. You're trying to hint there was something between us.'

'Was there?'

'I've had enough of this. Please leave.'

'I have more questions which need to be answered. I must remain here until they are. Do you agree you and Señor Gill had an affair?'

'No! Of course not.'

'Continue to deny this and I will have to continue questioning you when your husband has returned.'

'You can't.'

'I must.'

'You bastard!' she shouted.

'Tell me and since the señor is unfortunately dead, your husband will never know about the past unless you choose to tell him.'

She abruptly stood, crossed to the window, looked out. 'It's not true. But he might think . . . He's so . . .'

'The last thing I want is to bring trouble to your marriage.'

'I tell you, it's a horrible lie.'

'Yet you are scared of my talking to you in front of your husband.'

'He . . . he can be irrational.'

'And would be less sceptical than you'd want?'

They heard the slam of a car door. 'It's him,' she cried. Alvarez silently swore.

'Please. I beg you, don't say anything.'

He had hoped the threat to do so would have already forced her to speak the truth.

They heard Oakley enter the hall; the front door was slammed shut. There was the call: 'Virginia.'

She looked at Alvarez, frightened, fearful, desperate, silently pleading.

'Virginia.'

'In here,' she finally called out.

Oakley entered the room and came to a stop as he stared at Alvarez. 'Hullo, hullo, my wife entertaining a strange man whilst I'm away?'

There were times when the past was the present. Alvarez introduced himself.

'I confess, Inspector. I did rob the bank.' Oakley raised his hands in surrender. 'I didn't mean to shoot the manager, he just got in the way of me shooting the cashier.' He laughed and lowered his hands.

Alvarez understood why she had had an affair. Oakley enjoyed childish humour, possessed a beer belly which bulged over the top of his shorts and was partially visible through an unbuttoned shirt; he had little head hair, a plump, round face with small eyes and thick, rolling lips.

'The inspector . . .' she began, her voice uneven.

Alvarez hurriedly interrupted to prevent her trying to explain his presence. 'I'm here, señor, to ask what is the registration number of your car?'

'You speak-a da Eenglish!'

'I try to.'

'That's always good for a laugh. Had a waiter ask me if I wanted cut coffee. I said I'd have it in slices. Couldn't understand me . . . You want the number of my ancient Seat, Old Groaner. Can't remember the numbers, only the letters. They're a hoot. PIS. A man with a sense of humour handed them out, eh?'

'They mean nothing in Spanish.'

'Not much does. What's your name?'

'Inspector Alvarez.'

'You told me that. Not your surname, your Christian name.'

There was a silence.

'Wouldn't it be nice to offer the inspector a drink?' she asked.

'Drinking with the enemy! Not done, old girl, unless he's fought bravely.' He spoke to Alvarez. 'So what name will you answer to? Tony? What'll you drink, Tony? Arsenic with a touch of strychnine to add flavour?'

'Coñac with just ice, if I may?'

'This is freedom house and you take what you want in it.'

'Very generous.'

'I'd share the last penny in my pocket so long as I'd a few thousand quid in the bank.'

'I'd like a Cinzano,' she said, 'but I don't think there's any left.'

'Trust a woman to ask for something she can't have, eh, Tony?'

'Will you be a sweetie and go out and get me some?'

'There's sherry in the cupboard.'

'Just for once, can't you do as I ask?' She had spoken sharply when she had intended to speak sweetly.

'You'll have Tony thinking I never listen to you when in fact I spend all day rushing around, answering your every wish. It was me who should have vowed to honour and obey. I'll obey. Off to the corner shop for a bottle of Cinzano.' He left the room.

They heard a car door slam, an engine starting, the car driving away.

'Please, please don't tell him,' she pleaded. 'You've seen what he's like.'

'Did you have an affair with Señor Gill?'

'Yes,' she finally muttered. She looked at Alvarez to try to judge what impression her admission had made. 'Robin was so, so completely different. We met at a party. Paul had too much to drink, as always, and was being stupid, trying to impress Robin, laughing at his own jokes. Robin had the tact not to show his feelings . . .'

'Señora, we cannot have much time. Does your husband suspect you had an affair with Señor Gill?'

'Of course he doesn't.'

'How can you be so certain?'

'He's so fond of himself, he could hardly believe there was anyone I'd prefer to him. If he had become suspicious, he'd have been so humiliated, he'd have ordered me out of the house to live on charity since I wouldn't get a penny from him.'

They heard the car return.

'Please,' she pleaded.

Oakley entered, a plastic shopping bag in his hand. 'Bought a cream cake at the baker and told him the cream had better be fresh or I'd wash his face in it. Now, what was your order, Tony?'

'A coñac with just ice.'

'Service with a smile.' He crossed to the doorway, stopped, turned. 'You wanted to know the numbers of my car?'

'That's right.'

'Eight five three three. Can't think why you want to know?'

'There's been a road accident on the autoroute caused by a car doing well over a hundred and fifty. The passenger in the second car was not badly hurt and managed to take the registration number of the overtaking vehicle which drove off, but couldn't be certain of the last two numbers to identify them satisfactorily. We're questioning owners of cars to find out who it was.'

'Not guilty, m'lud. And if you don't believe me, go out and look at Old Groaner. If it could do a hundred and fifty, I'm the manager of Manchester United. And while you're looking, I'll pour a drink. A good stiff one, as the lady said to the barman.'

Alvarez was surprised Virginia had not found it preferable to live on charity.

NINE

Alvarez poured himself a drink. Alcohol calmed nerves, sharpened the mind, relaxed tension.

He finally phoned.

'Yes?' Angela Torres said with her usual brusqueness.

'Good afternoon, señorita. Can I speak to the superior chief?'

There was no answer.

'Dammit, isn't anyone there?' Salas demanded.

'Yes, señor.'

'Who are you?'

'Inspector Alvarez.'

'Then why in the devil didn't you tell my secretary who you were? Someone wanted to speak to me, she said, but had not identified himself. Am I supposed to guess who is calling?'

'She always knows who I am.'

'If that were so, she would not have referred to you as an unknown man. What do you want?'

'To make a report, señor.'

'Then why aren't you doing so?'

'I have questioned . . .'

'A report on what? Am I to guess that as well?'

'My investigation into the death of Señor Gill. I can be confident he did not commit suicide and Velaquez had nothing to do with that.'

'Your grounds for so assertive a conclusion?'

'Velaquez was in hospital at the time of the señor's death and, having reviewed the known and unknown facts, I questioned Señora Oakley.'

'Would it be too onerous for you to tell me who she is?'

'The wife of Señor Oakley.'

'Not a coincidence in names, then?'

'I don't understand, señor.'

'You have not explained who Mr and Mrs Oakley are, how they have any bearing on the case, and why it was important to question her.'

'I have mentioned her to you before, señor.'

'That precludes your making a full and proper report now? You take no account of the possibility I might have forgotten you had done so.'

'I presumed that was impossible.'

'Your presumption is unwelcome since I am trying once more to make you understand that when reporting . . . Perhaps I was being unrealistically ambitious. You will place the lady in context.'

'From what I learned, I believed Señora Oakley was having an affair with Señor Gill. I questioned her as to that. At first, she angrily denied the possibility, but finally I managed to make her admit it was true. I then questioned her closely to learn whether her husband could have suspected the relationship. She answered that was impossible since if he had believed it likely, or even possible, he would have thrown her out of the house.'

'It is unusual to hear of an Englishman who is ready to act honourably.'

'Hardly honourably, señor. She would then be without home or money.'

'An adulterous woman can expect nothing more.'

'But when she has . . .'

'You believe a husband should welcome his wife's adultery?'

'Señora Oakley has kept house for many years for a man you would not wish to marry under any circumstance.'

'You are amused to suggest I could consider marrying a man?'

'When I said "you", I did not mean you.'

'Were ambiguity to be welcomed, you would have made a success of your career.'

'I meant "you" was the average person.'

'One does not become superior chief by being average.'

'Of course not, señor.'

'There is no need to confirm the obvious.'

'Her evidence makes it impossible her husband had the slightest indication of what was going on which means, therefore, he had no reason to kill the dead man.'

'I find it extraordinary that I need constantly to remind you that one cannot kill a dead man.'

'I was using the term to identify Señor Gill.'

'Might not his name have done that more efficiently?'

'There is another point worth considering. If he had been responsible for Señor Gill's death, she would at least have suspected he was guilty. Then her contempt for him must have turned to hatred.'

'Would she have shown her hatred if she was terrified of being thrown out of the house?'

'She would have done so when speaking to me.'

'She would have attacked him in front of you?'

'Why do you suggest that?'

'How else could she have shown her anger as opposed to expressing it?'

'I . . . I questioned her concerning the señor's behaviour prior to his death to judge the possibility he was severely depressed despite what I had previously been told by others. She said he had behaved completely normally.'

'Who else has mentioned his behaviour?'

'The señorita, Parra and Luisa, the cook. The gardener suggested he might have been depressed, but my judgement of him is that he likes to twist things.'

'Hardly a useful trait for a gardener. You have made no mention of this before. You hold Gill did not commit suicide, and Oakley had no reason to murder him.'

'Yes, señor.'

'You do not allow that Oakley might have concealed his suspicions and Gill his depression?'

'That's unlikely.'

'Why?'

'In each case, après-ski would likely have resulted in their giving at least a hint of their true feelings.'

'Both men went skiing with the woman?'

'Hardly possible on this island.'

'You recognize that fact?'

'Après-ski is an expression.'

'Quite. Having completed their absurd pastime, the women parade, each one hoping her clothes are clearly more expensive than those of others.'

'It means something different to that.'

'You can explain what?'

'The time after. When one is completely relaxed and one often speaks without thought. Gill would admit to being depressed and his fears of the future. If suspicious, Oakley would persuade the señora to make damaging admissions.'

'The time after what?'

'You know.'

'On the contrary. I do not know, which is why I ask. Alvarez, do you remember my mentioning a friend, a noted psychiatrist who has become interested in your case. I need to speak again to him about you.'

'Señor, in this context, après-ski means . . .' Alvarez stopped. How to explain to someone who believed the primary purpose of a double bed was to sleep on it?

'Am I to be allowed to know what it means?'

'The period immediately after sex.'

There was a long pause.

'Alvarez, is your mind constantly occupied with the subject?'

'No, señor.'

'Yet were you in truth capable of ignoring your carnal interests, you might have undertaken the need to examine Gill's financial affairs.'

'I thought it best first to learn the truth from Señora Oakley.'

'Regrettably, that is now understandable. What is not, is your inability, before making this report, to tell me whether Señor Gill has lost large sums of money. Had he done so, the question of suicide must remain despite the opinion of others.'

'It was my intention to go to Aquila as soon as I finished reporting to you.'

'But now it is not?'

'Why do you ask?'

'Had the intention remained, you would have used the present tense, not the imperfect. Why have you delayed questioning Señorita Farren?'

'As I have mentioned, it would be kinder not to worry her further for the moment.'

'Is it your opinion she will be sufficiently calmed to be questioned before the end of the summer?'

'If you had been with me . . .'

'The case would have been handled efficiently.'

'I will be speaking to her tomorrow.'

'Unless you decide she is suffering from another crisis of nerves? You will observe the needs of the investigation, not the vapours of the lady who is the prime suspect and naturally taking full advantage of your weak naivety.'

The call finished. Prime suspect? The superior chief lacked all justification for calling her that. But how to prove this?

Alvarez said, as he reached across the dining-room table and picked up the bottle of Soberano, 'It's the weekend, yet I am having to work from dawn to long after dusk.'

Dolores came through the bead curtain. 'You demand sympathy?'

He poured out less brandy than he had intended for fear she would remind him that during the previous evening's television, a doctor had claimed that even a small amount of alcohol was dangerous to one's health. 'The seventh day is made for rest.'

'This is the sixth day.'

'But I've only just returned from work.'

'Work should cease midday Saturday and not resume until Monday morning?'

'Yes.'

'A decision I will observe. Each weekend, I will leave the house in the disorder in which I find it and I will do no cooking.'

'You . . . you can't,' Jaime spluttered.

'Why not?'

'What about us eating?'

'There is a stove in the kitchen and food to cook on it.'

'I don't know how to cook.'

'You will have a day and a half each weekend in which to learn.' She returned to the kitchen.

'Life wouldn't be so bloody difficult for everyone if people kept their big mouths shut,' Jaime said.

Had it not been a Sunday, Alvarez would have marked it a fine day at Aquila since there was a light breeze, giving the impression of less heat than below.

Parra opened the front door as he left the car. 'Good morning, Inspector. I hope all is well with you?'

'An impossibility. Is the señorita in?'

'I will find out if she is at home.'

Alvarez let his impatience surface. 'Forget the crap. Is she or isn't she here?'

'Perhaps you would like to come inside?'

That Parra was imitating the subservient servant of ancient times to annoy him, he accepted; and would have gained satisfaction from having just succeeded. In future, he would dent the other's malice by appearing to be friendly.

'You look grim,' Mary said, by way of greeting as he entered the sitting room. 'Is something wrong?'

'I was wishing I was not here.'

'That . . . that's not a very nice thing to say.'

'I would have been smiling broadly if my second reason for being here was not to ask more questions.'

'That's a relief and an irritation.'

He sat.

'Now you're here, I think you must redeem your promise.'

'Promise?'

'To have a Chinese meal with me.'

'I'm afraid my cousin is expecting me back to lunch,' he said hastily.

'Would it upset her very much to ask if she minds your staying here?'

There had been no indication of what Dolores was preparing for lunch. Sundays were often times at which she excelled herself. It was quite a while since she had cooked chuletas empapeladas, accompanied by a sauce devised by the gods. On the other hand, judging by her threats, she might be cooking something very ordinary, or even nothing.

'Forget it.'

Her disappointment was obvious and it might be the precursor to renewed depression. And Dolores, knowing his reason for being friendly with Mary, would understand his absence and not be annoyed by it. 'I was trying to remember whether my cousin will be home yet. Perhaps I could ring and find out?'

'There's a phone on the table.' She pointed to his right.

He picked up the cordless receiver, sat, dialled.

'Yes?' Dolores said.

'It's Enrique.'

'I am in the middle of cooking.'

'What work's that?'

'True! Cooking is work; cooking for men who think only of themselves is thankless work.'

With typical female blindness, she had failed to realize he had been trying to find out what she was cooking. The direct question in the hearing of Mary would be inadvisable since she might guess the reason. He would have to gamble. 'I wondered if you'd mind my not returning for lunch?'

'Of course I wouldn't.'

He was about to express his gratitude when she continued speaking.

'Why should it upset me that I have been slaving all morning in a furnace-hot kitchen in order to cook a meal which you do not want? If you have been offered dishes far superior to any I can prepare, of course you should enjoy them. What is not eaten here can be fed to the dog at the end of the road who might consider it edible.' She rang off.

'Is it all right?' Mary asked.

'Dolores doesn't mind.'

'I was only having cold meat and salad, so I'll tell Luisa there's a change of plan and we'll have Chinese takeaway. But first, which would you prefer – fried mice or pickled rat tails?' She laughed. 'If you could see your expression! You really thought that was a genuine choice, didn't you?'

He was glad temporarily to have afforded her some amusement, but did not regard the incident with the hilarity she did.

They had coffee, and he a cognac, in the library on the north side of the house, from which there was a view of the Tramuntana, lower than to the west, down to the port and beyond. One of the walls was lined with a bookcase, the shelves holding reference books, classic novels, and modern hardcovers in English and Spanish. To the right of the open fireplace hung two framed nonsense sketches by Heath Robinson, to the left was a large photograph of Aquila and Barca taken from the air. The kneehole desk was English, the two wooden and leather chairs and the carpet on the marble floor had been made locally. The bronze bust of a young woman was French. A pleasing meld of style.

'What exactly is it you want to know?' she asked, after Parra had collected the empty cups, saucers, and glasses.

'I'm afraid I have to learn what was your uncle's financial position. That means looking through his accounts, bank balances, and so on. I'll also need to read his will.'

'You still think he might have committed suicide?'

'I accept your judgement that that is impossible, but others won't until I can show it is too unlikely to be considered.'

'How he'd hate . . .'

He waited.

'Hate having anyone else look through all his papers. But I know you wouldn't unless you had to.'

'Your uncle was a very secretive man?'

'I don't know I'd call him that.' She stared into the past. 'He didn't want people to know what he owned, what he did, or what he really thought, but that was more maintaining his own self rather than being secretive. As far as I was concerned, from the moment I arrived here, he treated me as his daughter and answered whatever I wanted to know. But because I understood there were questions he disliked, such as any about his late wife, there were those I never asked.'

'Do you know the details of his will?'

'No. But he did say after I'd been here a while that he was glad I liked the place as much as he did, because one day it would be mine. It may still be so. I'm sure he'll have granted legacies to the servants. Beyond that, I've no idea.'

'There is a safe?'

'Behind the bookcase over there.' She pointed. 'Part of the bookcase is false.'

'Do you know where he kept the keys?'

'In one of the drawers of the desk.'

'I am going to have to look through the contents of the safe. If you can trust me on my own then . . .'

'Don't say that,' she said fiercely. 'I trust you completely.'

'Thank you. I was asking because it might be kinder for you not to be in here. Afterwards, I will show you anything you wish or need to see.'

She stood. 'You're right. I would start remembering . . . Call me if you need help.' She left.

There were two keys in the top right-hand drawer of the desk. The fake books in the bookcase were realistic until one studied them closely, knowing they were somewhere along the shelves. The safe was English and a small brass plaque claimed it to be both burglar and fireproof. Safe makers had to be optimistic. The keys turned the locks, and the thick, heavy door swung open. There was one shelf halfway up and on this was a wallet, several different-sized velvet covered boxes, passports for Gill and Mary, the new single-sheet residencias for them both, and various papers; there were more papers and several folders on the bottom of the safe. The wallet contained seven hundred euros in fifty-euro notes. The boxes contained many pieces of jewellery which, as far as his knowledge allowed him to judge, were very valuable. He returned the jewellery and wallet to the shelf, brought out the contents, placed them on the desk.

Gill's paperwork had been left in good order. There were folders marked investments, credits, outgoings. There were statements from banks in Mallorca, England, and Liechtenstein, all showing healthy credits. There was an IOU, signed by Timothy Kiernan, for 10,000 pounds. Gill's will, in Spanish and English, was in one folder. His estate was left to Mary Farren, subject to payments of legacies. These were 1500 pounds to Parra, Luisa, and Santos, 1000 pounds to Eva, and 10,000 pounds to Miranda Pearson.

Using the calculator on the desk, he made a quick estimate of the worth of the estate. Roughly thirty thousand in the banks. The latest investment report totalled 1,876,000. The property? A million.

He leaned back and gazed into a life of millions of euros. A farm, around a hundred hectares. Considerably larger than usual in the area, but not impossible. A finca, to let to tourists, not to live in – there was not wealth sufficient to forgo Dolores' cooking. A large flock of red sheep, now not quite so close to extinction since the government had seen the wisdom of granting subsidies to promote their breeding. Many pigs. No animal was the equal of a pig in the kitchen. Chorizo, sobresada, botifarró; chops, legs, trotters, tongue; ham and hamon serano. Cows? Fresh milk was a different liquid from that which one bought in cartons and which was fortified, skimmed, pasteurized, and heaven knew what else. But cows had to be milked twice a day. Hire a cowman.

Regretfully, he returned to the world he lived in. He collected things together, returned them to the safe, locked that, swung the section of false bookcase back into position. In the last investment analysis, his account executive had written that markets had been volatile and Gill's holdings had inevitably suffered, but the losses had been less than those of the general market. The outlook was uncertain, but there was good reason to think that in relative terms, the investments would remain firm.

Gill, suffering from no fatal disease or mental problem, living in luxury, rich enough to survive a worldwide financial crisis, enjoying at least one loving mistress, was going to commit suicide? Even Salas would accept that he was not.

In the sitting room, Mary was knitting. She looked up, said 'Damn!' and looked back down at the knitting, fiddled with the needles.

'Lost a stitch?' he asked.

'Two.'

He sat. 'Do you do a lot of knitting?'

'What else is there for an oldie to do but that and watch the telly?'

'I'll never see a younger oldie.'

'How do you manage always to say the right thing?'

He smiled.

'Have I said something amusing?'

'Many people would suggest I never manage to say the right thing.'

'Then they don't know you.' She had regained the stitches and started another row. 'I'm making a baby jacket for the wife where I get the Sunday papers and quite often a daily one. She told me what was very obvious and is worried because her husband isn't well and she has to be in the shop all day, every day, and there isn't the time to prepare for the coming baby. I said she should close in the after-noons and evenings, and she said she's not allowed to. Is that right?'

'Newsagents have to be open all day, every day. That law was meant to encourage people to read.'

'Surely, there isn't anyone now who doesn't? So why not relax the law?'

'Politicians don't worry about the effects of the laws they promulgate unless they become involved in the conse-quences. And when you say everyone now is literate, that's almost true but, not so many years ago, some people had to give their fingerprint instead of a signature at a bank because they could not write.'

'Then there's been real progress.'

'I suppose so.'

'Why the doubt?'

'Years ago, the elderly were cared for by their children, drugs were virtually unknown, houses were affordable, every possible square metre of land was cultivated and did not grow thistles and brambles.'

'You'd like the country to be back in those days?'

'When there was hunger, when one could not afford a

visit to a doctor, and when one endured toothache because there was no dentist within a mule ride? Sadly, it seems there can never be a world that is all light, there has to be a matching darkness . . . I am talking too much and boring you.'

'That you are not. And you have to keep talking to tell me what you've learned.'

'The señor's will provides several legacies, otherwise you inherit the estate. A large sum of money is involved and I advise you to speak to a top tax adviser in Palma in order to escape the shark jaws of the tax inspectors. Left unchallenged, they will strip a person of every last euro.'

'Can you suggest someone?'

'I will find out who can be most trusted to act for you, not the government. There is something more. You know there is considerable jewellery in the safe?'

'It was Robin's wife's. She inherited some of it, Robin gave her the rest. He wanted me to have it, but if I wore such beautiful things . . .' She stopped abruptly.

She might have told him he said the right thing at the right time, but now he could think of nothing to say. To wear such glittering beauty would be to exacerbate the misfortune of her deformity; it would attract the unwanted attention of men. 'I would judge the jewellery to be very valuable; at a quick glance, none of it appeared to be imitation.'

'It isn't. Robin had a hatred of anything false which tried to make out it was genuine. The reproduction Hepplewhite presented as original. It was the same with people. If someone genuinely needed help, he would give it. If they did so just because he was wealthy, he would have no truck with them. He was like that with the Phillipses. I sometimes wondered if he'd been tricked by a so-called friend when young.'

'Who are they?'

'Live in one of the biggest houses, drive a Rolls and get stuck in the village corners, own a large motor yacht, frequently go on world cruises in one of the top suites. Quite a few people here live that kind of life, but most of them do so unostentatiously. Meet the Phillipses and within minutes you learn they're very wealthy, had noble ancestors who left them their seat in one of the shires, would be on every A-list of celebrities had they wished to be. At the same time, they are contemptuous of "little people", by which they mean those who have small houses or live in a village, whose accent is often described as uneducated, who have to watch every euro. When a firm does badly, there are redundancies and people appear on television saying they don't know how they can manage with mortgages, credit card debts, and so on, Frank Phillips will say they should stop bleating and think themselves lucky they aren't thrown into a debtors' prison.'

'Sympathetic!'

'Robin disliked them within minutes of meeting them. Dislike became anger when they were so damned rude to friends. George and Lilly Carson are short of money and have to cut corners, but you never hear them complain. Phillips had asked them to one of their ostentatious parties. Lilly rang us to say Frank had just been in touch to tell them he'd invited too many people so they were not to come. The not-so-rich or the unimportant were being discarded.

'Robin said no one with manners and education could act like that and they had to be fakes. He'd find out who they really were. I thought he was just talking until he spoke to Alec, a retired detective, and hired him to dig out the truth.

'It took time, but in the end we learned her name was Gertrude, not Guinevere, none of their ancestors had ever owned a large estate, a small estate, or anything better than a back-to-back, and Frank had made his money from pornography.

'Had the information just been sufficient to burst the bubble of falsity, Robin would probably have leaked it, but as things turned out, he decided it would be too unkind to release the truth. We would have our private laugh when the Phillipses boasted about the grand family estate they had inherited. However, the news escaped. That had to be through Alec who probably at some time had been at the receiving end of the Phillips' snobbery.'

'Have they stayed on the island?'

'Surprisingly. I suppose one should give them slight credit for facing all the jeering laughter behind their backs. Robin has a strange sense of humour . . .' She stopped. 'Had,' she murmured. She looked away from him and it was a while before she continued speaking. 'What started in fun, ended bitterly.'

'As we say, if you don't know where the journey will end, don't saddle up.'

'It's easy to be wise afterwards.'

'I wasn't criticizing your uncle.'

She put knitting and needles into a wicker basket. 'It sounded as if you were.'

'Then I'm sorry.'

'You think I'm being bitchy?'

'No.'

'It's just . . .'

He accepted she was ready to find insult and criticism when not intended because grief sometimes provoked that need. He hoped a return to other matters would calm her. 'As you said, the keys to the safe were in a drawer in the desk. They're dangerously accessible and probably a desk drawer would be the first place where a thief would look. It would be a good idea to hide them very carefully, away from the library.'

'You're worried someone might break in to the house?'

'Yes. And there could be a closer worry.'

'How d'you mean?' Her expression sharpened. 'Are you suggesting the staff would steal?'

'The jewellery is insured for tens of thousand of pounds.'

'Pablo, Luisa, Eva, or Juanito wouldn't touch an uncounted pile of a hundred euro notes. You just can't understand loyalty. For you, everybody is a potential thief. I wonder who I am in that mind of yours?'

'Someone who has had to suffer too much,' he answered quietly. He stood. 'Thank you for your help.'

'Enrique . . .'

He remained standing where he was.

'I didn't mean that. But I couldn't bear your being suspicious of them when they've been so kind to me.'

'I have no reason to suspect them, but I have met one or two people whose characters have been changed and ruined by money. If the keys are well hidden, your faith and my worries will be guarded.'

'Very well. I'll do as you suggest, not that I think it can possibly be necessary, but because you want it.'

'Peace is declared?'

'Did I sound as if war had begun?'

'Which I provoked . . . There is one more question.'

'Yes?'

'Do you know Miranda Pearson?'

'No. Should I?'

'She has been left ten thousand pounds.'

She said nothing.

He looked at his watch. 'I really must leave, much as I'd like to stay.'

'You've lost your nerve?'

'In what way?'

'You are having lunch here.' She laughed. 'Now I know how a man looked when asked to dine with a de' Medici. But before anything else . . .'

He waited.

'I've been told the funeral can now take place.'

'Will you be on your own?'

'Luisa and Pablo will be with me.'

'Good.'

'I've arranged for a cremation.'

Something of which the average Mallorquin disapproved. Without a grave, how could one been seen regularly to lay flowers on it, showing the dead was not forgotten. He spoke carefully. 'I think after the funeral you will be able to accept an end and this will afford some relief.'

'Does it?'

'I found it so.' A relief from harsh mental pain, but not from sorrow – that might never end.

TEN

'You have carried out my orders?' Salas asked over the phone.

'Yes, señor.'

'But have not seen fit to make a report.'

'There's been so much to do.'

'Were I to accept your words without reservation, I could enjoy the picture of your working hard. Have you questioned Señorita Farren?'

'At considerable length.'

'You were able to overcome your sympathy for her emotional state?'

'Yes.'

There was a silence.

'Despite working so hard, you have learned nothing?'

'On the contrary, I have learned several important facts.'

'Am I to be permitted to learn what those are?'

'The señorita gave me permission to open the señor's safe . . . Or should I say, the señorita's safe? The estate has been left to her, so I suppose the safe and its contents are now hers. I have read copies of his will – one is in English, one is in Spanish.'

'Did you compare them to make certain the details are similar?'

'Yes.'

'What are the main details?'

'As I have mentioned, the señorita is left the estate, subject to certain legacies. I have made a rough estimate of the capital. The total is very nearly two million pounds, the jewellery is insured for seventy-five thousand. Then there's the house and land. I suppose that would be worth close on another million euros to someone who does not suffer from altophobia.'

'Who can control his own mind. The will clearly provides

the motive for murder and potential identification of the prime suspect.'

'Are you suggesting Señorita Farren again? That is . . .' He stopped.

'You wish to complete your sentence?'

'It is the possibility, señor, which is unlikely. In no circumstances would I refer to a decision of yours as ridiculous.'

'You have not previously done so?'

'The legacies provide fifteen hundred pounds for three of the staff, a thousand for the fourth. The question raised is, could these relatively small sums provoke murder? On the face of things, almost certainly not. And how could any member of the staff know the details of the will when it was in the safe? Yet the keys were easily accessible.'

'My understanding of what you have said is that they might or they might not, which has the benefit of being a logical, if useless, conclusion.'

'The keys of the safe were left in a drawer of the desk in the library. A member of the staff might well have discovered them there, opened the safe, and read the will. Which raised further questions. Would not he, or she, also have stolen something from the contents? Cash or a little jewellery. Again, why would the thief be such a fool as to imagine he, or she, could sell something of such quality without drawing attention to himself or herself? Would the risk of discovery not militate against theft since that would ensure the loss of the legacy.'

'Have you concluded your summary of probabilities, possibilities, and impossibilities?'

'Yes, señor.'

'I am grateful.'

'There is a further bequest of ten thousand pounds to Miranda Pearson. This raises the question . . .'

'Restrict yourself to answers.'

'Señorita Farren has never heard the señora's name mentioned. I think it probable she is an old friend and the gift was for services rendered.'

'You consider friendship to be a service?'

'Very close friends.'

'There is significance in the addition?'

'Señor, one does not leave a large sum of money to a woman who is unknown to the family unless there has been a close relationship which is remembered with pleasure or reproachful guilt.'

'And which would you choose?'

'Perhaps both.'

'Naturally. My friend, the eminent psychiatrist, will be interested in this latest evidence of satyriasis.'

'I have learned that there exist motives for murder other than money, although one of them is concerned with money.'

'It might add verisimilitude to your report if you do not continually contradict yourself. Either what you are about to say is concerned with money, or it is not.'

'In amongst the papers in the safe was an IOU for ten thousand pounds, signed by Timothy Kiernan. If Kiernan has not been in a position to repay this considerable sum, he may have decided to cancel the debt physically.'

'Leaving the IOU in the safe to inculpate himself?'

'He may claim he repaid the debt, but Señor Gill had forgotten to destroy the IOU.'

'Such claim can be rebutted by examining the bank balances of Señor Gill, as you will do.'

How many hours work would that involve? 'Señor, the sum may have been paid in cash which was not put into a bank . . .'

'No man in his right senses keeps thousands of pounds or euros in cash.'

'You have not heard of Old Jacobo Martinez. He was a recluse.'

'Then I am hardly likely to have heard of him.'

'When he died, there were a hundred and forty thousand pesetas hidden in a box in his tumbledown caseta.'

'One would expect an Englishman to have more intelligence than a Mallorquin peasant. And the payee would have demanded the IOU in order to destroy it.'

'One should also consider whether it might be a hoax.'

'What impossibility are you proposing now?'

'As a joke, Señor Gill might have made out the IOU and

signed it with the name of Kiernan, shown it to friends and complained he had not been repaid.'

'Then his mind must be on a par with that of the man who can think up such a possibility.'

'His niece described him as having a puckish sense of humour.'

'Does she know what humour means?'

'He was clearly an unusual man. And his character provides another possible motive for his death. Señorita Farren explained that he had a very strong aversion to fakes; things which were presented as what they were not . . .'

'Such as inspectors?' Salas suggested.

'People who tried to make out they were much grander than they were. There's an English couple, Phillips, who live in the area. Apparently, they present themselves as being very well connected, they inherited a large country property which they sold and explains their wealth, and because of their supposed superior background, do not like to acknowledge those they consider to be "little people".'

'Such traits distinguish them from many of their compatriots?'

'Señor Gill was convinced they were frauds. And when they were very rude to his friends, he decided to find out if he was right. He hired a retired English detective to uncover their true background.

'He learned the Phillipses were of plebeian ancestry and had not inherited a large country estate. He had made his money from pornography.'

'Your interest is explained.'

'Señor Gill had never intended the information to become known to others, but through no fault of his, it did. When the Phillipses understood they were being viewed with derision instead of envy, it must have been like a draught of poison. The cloak had been lifted to reveal them naked.'

'You lack sufficient artistic talent to talk nonsense.'

'Señor Phillips must have been determined to get his own back.'

'You are presenting that as a motive for Señor Gill's murder?'

'Yes, señor.'

'Extremely weak.'

'I disagree. Would you not feel so angry, you'd want to revenge yourself if someone was responsible for making it known that you had only been promoted superior chief because you had a powerful relative in the government and that you led a luxurious life because on the side, you ran a brothel?'

'Your insolence has gone too far.'

'I am merely trying to explain why I consider Phillips had sufficient reason to murder Señor Gill.'

'Arrant hypocrisy.'

'Surely no one in high authority would accept that a mere inspector would dare to make the false accusation that his senior would seek promotion by the back door or that he had ever stepped into a brothel, let alone run one? It is against all experience and common sense; a sparrow does not challenge an eagle.'

'It pleases you to indulge in feather-brained stupidity?' Salas said, before ringing off.

Alvarez stepped into the entrada, determined to gird up his loins like a man. Unfortunately, he felt ungirded.

In the sitting room, Jaime sat at the table, bottle and glass in front of himself. Alvarez sat and brought a glass out of the sideboard. Something worried him until he realized no sounds came from the kitchen. 'Isn't she here again?' He poured himself a drink.

'Went out to buy something she needed. Wanted me to get it. Like I told her, shopping is a woman's job.'

'You said it in those words?'

'Maybe not exactly.'

'Was she annoyed when I rang to say I couldn't get back to lunch?'

'Kept on about feeding the dogs. I told her, it was me who wanted something to eat.'

'What was the meal?'

'Can't rightly remember . . . Why do you keep annoying her?' Jaime asked, with sudden anger. 'Then it's me who gets it in the neck. I don't do this, I don't do that. Women can't understand a man needs to rest when he gets back worn out from work.'

Alvarez produced a packet of Ducados and offered it.

'They're the best you could get?'

'The best I could afford, not being a politician on the fiddle.'

Jaime drew a cigarette out of the pack. As he struck a match and held it out for Alvarez, he heard the front door open. He hurriedly refilled his glass with his free hand.

Dolores came through from the entrada. She spoke to Alvarez. 'We are to have the pleasure of your company at supper?'

'I'm sorry about lunch . . .'

'Was it the President of the Commission who could not be denied your presence at lunch?' She swept into the kitchen and banged a saucepan to express her feelings.

'She's in another mood because of you,' Jaime muttered.

Alvarez wondered if sweet words might lessen her annoyance? He went through to the kitchen. 'I'm very sorry, but I didn't know what I should do.'

'Even when a man does, he doesn't do it.' She began to shell peas.

'Naturally I wanted to return, but I felt I had to stay and give what little help I could.'

'She needed her back covered in suntan cream?'

'Who do you think I was with?'

'A young woman, probably English or French, insufficiently experienced to realize that the interest of a much older man is not paternal in nature.'

'I was with Mary Farren at Aquila. I had to question her again which made her very depressed. I felt guilty because of this and when she asked me to stay, I decided I simply had to provide what comfort I could. There are times when one has to sacrifice oneself.'

'Why did you not explain when you phoned me?'

'She would have heard what I said. Had she known I was staying against my wish, was doing so only for her sake, she would have become even more depressed.'

She began to fine-chop three teeth of garlic.

'Would you have had me desert her at such a time?'

'You ask a foolish question. Did she offer you food?'

'Yes.'

'Was it a reasonable meal?'

'Sadly, I had to eat a Chinese takeaway.'

She carefully added the garlic to the contents of an earthenware pot. 'I have heard there are such things for foreigners.'

'Mallorquins eat them.'

'In preference to a meal cooked at home?'

'Not everyone is so dedicated to the family as you are.'

'Perhaps. But then I was brought up to believe, mistakenly, that a woman's pleasure was to ensure the family was content. Of course, in those days there were men who still understood the meaning of gratitude.'

'Jaime and I can't sufficiently express our gratitude for all you do for us.'

'Which is, perhaps, why you never do.' She lowered the gas under the pot. 'You enjoyed this meal?'

'How could I when I was missing the meal cooked by you. Perhaps supper will compensate me?'

'It is nothing special. But maybe for lunch tomorrow, I will cook Ternera a la Jardinera.'

Veal, stock, ham, shallots, carrots, potatoes, peas and spices. On paper, a mere recipe, in truth, a gourmet's dream. He expressed his delight at the prospect. He returned to the sitting room, picked up his glass and drank. In the kitchen, Dolores began to sing about a young woman whose young man had returned from afar and finally made his feelings known.

'She's calmed right down as you can hear. It's thanks to what I told her,' Alvarez said.

'You wouldn't need to say anything if you came back here when you should,' Jaime said ill-temperedly.

The gateway might have been guarding a castle rather than a very large, modern house of little visual charm; the garden was extensive, but too well manicured and a waste of land since only flowers and shrubs were grown; the infinity swimming pool seemed almost of an infinite size; in front of the garage was a Jaguar, and visible inside, a Volvo. At least there was no helicopter landing pad.

Alvarez climbed the four tiled steps, stepped into the pillared patio and activated the bell push to the right of the panelled wooden front door. This was opened by a man in his late thirties who wore the traditional white shirt and dark trousers of service. He studied Alvarez, noted the well-worn clothing, the unshaven chin, and his expression pictured the contempt a servant in a rich home often had for a member of the proletariat. 'Yes?'

'Is Señor Phillips here?' Alvarez asked in Mallorquin.

There was a slight pause. 'I do not know if he is at home.'

'Then you can find out.'

There was a call in English. 'Who is it, Joders?'

'I am about to find out, señor,' he answered in the same language.

An internal door was shut.

'If that was Señor Phillips, you don't need to find out if he is in.'

'It will be best if you leave.'

'Best for whom?'

'Do you want trouble?'

'I am always meeting trouble from Mallorquins who have learned their manners from foreigners. My name is Inspector Alvarez, Cuerpo General de Policia.'

'I fear I didn't recognize you, Inspector. If you had said who you were . . .'

'You would not have decided I was a mendicant? As I said, I want to speak to Señor Phillips.'

'Of course, Inspector. Please come into the green room and I will tell the señor you are here.'

The hall was large and over-furnished; the green room was not very green and expensively over-furnished. Through the windows, the mountains were visible – with the bright sunshine covering them, they appeared light grey, speckled with the green of pine trees which performed the impossible by growing on their slopes.

Phillips entered the room. He spoke pugnaciously in English, his voice carrying clipped tones as he spoke with care. 'Joders says you're some sort of policeman. What brings you here?'

He was a large man with a round, sharply featured face, a mouth which looked hard enough to crack walnuts, square shoulders, broad chest, only the hint of a stomach, and hairy legs below the shorts.

The delay in an immediate answer annoyed Phillips. 'You don't understand English. Typical! None of you people do.'

He decided not to point out that in Spain, one spoke Castilian, Catalan, Galician, Euskara or Mallorquin. 'I speak a little English, señor.'

'Then you can explain why you're interrupting my morning?'

'I wish to ask you some questions.'

'Some other time. I have guests.'

'I fear it must be now.'

'What the devil! You come here and think you can order me about?'

He did think so and it would be a pleasure. Phillips not only considered he was speaking to a man from an inferior race, he was also a natural bully. 'I have questions which you will need to answer.'

'Don't think you can speak to me like that . . .' Phillips stopped as his wife entered.

'Marcelo told me someone was here.' She studied Alvarez.

'We are not on Christian-name terms with our servants.'

'It seems more friendly.'

'They are not paid for their friendship.'

Alvarez coughed to remind them he was present.

'Is he . . . ?'

'Says he's some sort of policeman.'

'Something's wrong?'

She was younger than her husband by many years. Her black hair was styled, her make-up possessed the quality of not being apparent, even to his ignorant eyes, her dress was of top quality, the diamond brooch on her right bosom sparkled as she moved, and the diamond of her engagement ring in size matched many of those in the safe at Aquila. 'I am here to ask a few questions, señora.'

'I'll handle this,' Phillips said. 'There's no need to stay. Best get back to Bill and Thelma.'

She left.

'Are you going to explain why you wish to ask questions?' Phillips demanded.

'Have you heard about the unfortunate death of Señor Gill?'

'Naturally. With all the tittle-tattle, how could I not?'

'Although his death might have been an accident, there is now reason to believe it might not.'

'You are trying to say he was murdered?'

'At the moment, that is possible.'

'But, typically, you don't know.'

'Matters are not straightforward.'

'They never are on this island. You still haven't explained why you're here.'

'We're speaking to people who may be able to help us determine the cause of his death.'

'Fell a couple of hundred feet on to rock. That is not cause enough? You're wasting my time by coming here.'

'Why is that?'

'I have no idea how or why he died?'

'But you had reason to dislike him.'

'Ridiculous! Do you mind leaving right away?'

'I have more questions.'

'I have just explained why any question to me is meaningless.'

'In the past, you were very rude to his friends.'

'This is becoming farcical.'

'You invited Señor and Señora Carson to a party, then rang them to say you'd asked too many people and they were not to come.'

'What if I did?'

'You cannot understand they were insulted?'

'They were lucky to be invited in the first case. Making up numbers.'

'Señor Gill was troubled by your action.'

'None of his damned business.'

'To him, it showed you were not the person you tried to make out you were.'

'I am not going to listen to any more of this nonsense. Clear out of my house.'

'I will leave when I am finished.'

'If you're still here in a couple of minutes, I'll have the staff throw you out.'

'You will find them very unwilling to do so, as you should be.'

'You'd better understand I'm very friendly with many important people.'

'However important, they will not interfere with a judicial investigation. Is it fact that Señor Gill learned you had not inherited a large estate which you sold very profitably, you had made your money from pornography?'

'A vicious lie.'

'Señor Gill had not intended the facts to become public because he was too good-natured to wish on you the derision and contempt they must cause. But the facts were broadcast by someone else. You thought you had reason to hate Señor Gill.'

'Who's been telling you all these damned lies? That half-witted niece who runs if you get near her?'

'You are referring to Señorita Farren? Your judgement is as erroneous as it is slanderous.'

'You think I'll have a village policeman talk to me like that?'

'I thought I had already done so. And I have not finished. Can you explain why, if you did inherit your wealth and did not make it from pornography, you did not take legal steps to squash the rumour?'

'I don't give a damn what the cloth-caps think.'

'Because of the circumstances, I will speak to the English police and ask them to confirm or deny what you claim. Should they find you were lucratively engaged in the pornographic trade, they may be interested in knowing whether you declared your income to the tax officials and how you transferred so large a sum here, as you must have done.

Was it moved legally or illegally, since you did not wish there to be evidence of your earnings? Where were you on Friday, the fourth of this month?'

'I don't know or bloody well care.'

'It is in your interests to be concerned if you do not wish to be suspected of the death of Señor Gill.'

'This is too absurd to be possible.'

'I should like an answer?'

'You'll wait a goddam long time.'

'Señor, would you prefer to be brought to the post in Llueso?'

'You . . . You'd arrest me? Me?' Phillips' emotion had become bewildered surprise. A varlet threatening the lord of the manor?

Alvarez finally said: 'You will report to the Guardia post in Llueso – which is where I work – at eighteen hundred hours this afternoon.'

'Like hell I will.'

'If you are not there by eighteen thirty, I will send two policia to escort you.'

The door opened and Gertrude Phillips entered. 'How much longer are you going to be? Thelma's wondering what you're up to and I can't tell her the police are here or she'll spread even worse rumours than she usually does.'

'He . . . he's threatening to arrest me.'

'Nonsense!'

'Señora, if your husband persists in refusing to answer me, he must come to the post, either on his own or in the company of the policia. Even English gentlemen have to obey Spanish law.'

'I intend to report you for your ridiculous and insulting behaviour.'

'Your complaint may bring joy to my superior, but it cannot alter the need for the señor to answer me.'

'What is the question?'

'Where was your husband on the fourth of this month?'

'Valletta.'

'In Malta?'

'You imagine it to be in Katmandu?'

He spoke to Phillips. 'Can you prove you were there at that date?'

'You think I'm lying?' she demanded shrilly.

'You could be, señora.'

'Did you hear that? He called me a liar.'

'No,' Alvarez contradicted. 'I merely observed that it had to be possible.'

'Don't you argue with me. I heard you. It's quite outrageous.'

'You are excited, señora, so it will be best if I leave. Señor, you will be at the post at eighteen hundred hours.'

Phillips muttered, 'Anything to end this farce. We were on a short Mediterranean cruise.'

'You can prove that?'

'Are you calling him a liar as well?' she screamed. 'Frank, call the consul and tell him we're being victimized by the local police.'

'I'd better show him what we have.'

'Ignore him.'

'It may succeed in his leaving.'

She flounced out of the room.

Minutes later, Alvarez was shown the receipt for the cost of the cruise, a couple of dated menus, and a receipt for money changed in Malta.

ELEVEN

Phone to his ear, Alvarez waited. The day was hotter than ever, and the fan was turning at its quickest yet offering little relief; the promised installation of air-conditioning had never happened. As always, a bureaucratic promise was just words.

Typically, Salas did not bother to offer a pleasant greeting. 'Yes?'

'I have just spoken to Señor Phillips, señor.'

'Who is I?'

Alvarez wondered if the superior chief was beginning to suffer from mental problems. 'I think you are Superior Chief Salas.'

'You negate the belief that speech enables there to be mutual comprehension. What the devil do you mean by that?'

'But you said, "Who is I?"'

'If, for some totally obscure reason I had been asking you who I was, I would have said, "Who am I?" A moment of common sense would have told you that I was attempting, yet again, to make you understand that you should have identified yourself.'

'In the past, you have blamed me for wasting your time by giving my name when your secretary had already told you who was phoning.'

'And if she was unable to do so, I would know who was calling by telepathy?'

'She forgot?'

'Try not to judge others by yourself. Before she could inform me, something occurred with which she had to deal immediately. Explain why you are phoning and start at the beginning, not the middle or the end.'

'I have been questioning Señor Phillips. Initially he was very obstructive, as was his wife. They thought because they were English, they did not have to observe the laws of Spain.'

'You made their error very clear?'

'Yes, señor. And this had the effect of causing them to become aggressively rude although he has claimed to be a gentleman.'

'That gave reason to be surprised?'

'They are known to be very well mannered.'

'Pure myth.'

'They were also completely honest. Hence, the word of an English gentleman. Perhaps since the invasion by the tourists that has little meaning, but before then, it was used and accepted as an unbreakable promise.'

'Has there ever been such a thing on this island?'

'Have you not heard of the Duc de Mora?'

'No. And you will not . . .'

'He lived in the days when a great landowner had almost total authority over his tenants. The Duc had invited an English milord, who spoke good Castilian, but no Mallorquin since that was not for milords, to his grand mansion. But the Duc was suddenly ordered to Madrid and when the English milord arrived, he was not there. The staff explained what had happened and that the Duc hoped the Englishman would remain as he expected to return very soon. The Englishman might have been a milord, but he had a heart. One day, he was walking when he saw a young woman weeping as she used a mattock to make irrigation channels in the soil. He asked her what was the matter. She knew she should be silent because the Duc would be furious to learn she had spoken, but she could not remain quiet. The Duc had accepted her father as a new tenant and had very recently seen her for the first time. He told her she was beautiful, like a virginal rose, and she must join the staff in the mansion and not lose her beauty working on the land in the sun, wind, and rain. She knew what that meant – he would seduce her and then cast her aside. Because the Duc was a man who always had what he wanted, she could be certain that if she defied him, he would throw her father off the land. Times were very hard, the land was still in the hands of very wealthy men, so it would be almost impossible for her father to find another tenancy. Her family would be reduced to starvation. To save them, she must sacrifice herself; but then she would never marry because she would have become dishonoured.

'The milord was horrified by what she said. He told her to cease weeping; he would buy land, his father could farm it as his tenant, and she need not fear the Duc. Her mother was certain the milord was filling her daughter's mind with fools' dust. He would not buy any land, would wait until her father had forgone his tenancy, then would say that unless her daughter responded to his disgusting desires, they would be left to starve. But the father believed the milord and left the Duc's tenancy. The milord bought fifty hectares of good land, the father became his tenant and more successful than he could ever have hoped to be. The milord demanded nothing from the daughter; indeed, he gave her a very handsome present when she married a good, working lad. That is why to promise on the word of an English gentleman used to be as binding as an oath made on the bible.'

'Alvarez, you wasted a great deal of my time with a story intended for children. Had you known anything about the English aristocracy, you would appreciate such an offer would never have been made disinterestedly. Have you anything of interest to say?'

'I have a report to make, señor.'

'Then make it without any reference to fairy godfathers.'

'I have questioned Señor and Señora Phillips who were aggressively rude.'

'Is it necessary to repeat what you have already said?'

'He denied there was any truth in his ever having been engaged in pornography. One has to accept he might be telling the truth and Señor Gill made up the story to avenge his friends, but from what I've learned about Señor Gill, he would never have acted like that. Had he wanted to make fun of Phillips, rather than uncover the truth, he would have thought up something witty . . .'

'Do you, or do you not, believe Phillips was a pornographer?'

'I don't know.'

'Why not?'

'To be certain, one would need help from the English police since the evidence of dealings in pornography will be there. However, there is no reason to bother them. Señor Phillips and his wife were able to prove that at the time of Señor Gill's death, they were on a Mediterranean cruise and had landed at Valletta.'

'Making nonsense of your theory that he had a motive for murder. A mistaken possibility funded by an overactive and unrealistic imagination instead of intelligent logic.'

'Yet by establishing he has this alibi, I have reduced the possible number of suspects.'

'It would have shown a more alert intelligence had you tried to name the guilty party rather than establishing innocence.'

'Yet by eliminating him . . .'

'Do you remember what I said at the beginning of this investigation?'

'With reference to what?'

'Money. In this case, there is a considerable amount which offers a prime motive. Who benefits financially from the death of the señor?'

'The staff have been left small amounts and Miranda Pearson a larger one.'

'That is all?'

'Apart from Kiernan who may have hoped to delete his debt.'

'Does Señorita Farren not inherit the whole estate less the bequests?'

'But . . .' Alvarez stopped abruptly.

'You wish to insult me again?'

'Señor, remembering how much she inherits, it may seem logical to consider her as the possible prime suspect, but she did not kill her uncle.'

'Your proof?'

'It is very difficult to prove a negative, as you have told me in the past. But her grief on learning of her uncle's death . . .'

'Assumed grief is one of women's favourite defences.'

'She was grieving hysterically.'

'Hysterics is another.'

'I am certain she had no part in her uncle's death.'

'Your judgement lacks all weight, remembering your certainty Señor Phillips had so strong a motive. You will find out from the staff if there were signs of friction between her and her uncle, in particular because she had become involved with a man whom Señor Gill disliked so much that he threatened to disinherit her if she continued to see the man.'

'That is most unlikely. Señorita Farren can not bear to have a man touch her.'

'Have you disgraced the cuerpo by making what I believe is called a pass, and rightly have been contemptuously rejected?'

'She informed me of the fact.'

'Which will be because you had given reason.'

'When I told her about the death of her uncle, she was in a terrible state and I tried, as one does, to comfort her by briefly touching her.'

'A man of honour does not for any reason touch a woman he hardly knows.'

'On this island, señor . . .'

'There are very few men of honour. You will find out if she is involved with a man, if her uncle disliked him and threatened to disinherit her if the relationship continued.'

'Señor, you have been upbraiding me for suggesting imaginative motives, yet what you have just proposed is not imaginative, it is impossible.'

The line became dead.

Alvarez left the post, made his way across the square in which people joked and laughed because they were not subject to a tyrannical boss, and went into Club Llueso.

'You're a stranger at this time of the day,' was Roca's greeting. 'Been given the sack?'

'That would almost be a pleasure. Give me a large coñac.'

* * *

Alvarez entered the dining room. Isabel and Juan were watching the television, Jaime, at the table, looked up. 'You're in time, then.'

'For what?'

'She was beginning to worry you'd be so late, she'd have to dish up before you returned.'

Alvarez poured himself a drink. 'I wonder what she's cooked. With the kind of day I'm having, it'll be something ordinary.'

Dolores stepped through the bead curtain. 'You're late.'

'I had endless work to finish.'

'In which bar? As you have finally arrived, we can eat. I've had to keep the meal warm when it needed to be served immediately, which won't have improved it.'

Juan looked away from the television to speak to his mother. 'Uncle won't mind.'

'Indeed!'

'He said the meal will only be something very ordinary.'

'It is always interesting to learn how one's work is appreciated.'

Alvarez spoke hastily. 'I only . . .'

'Of course, I understand that my meals are not to be compared to those available at a Chinese takeaway.'

'All I said was, because I've had such a terrible day . . .'

'Mine, of course, has been easy since I only had to make beds, collect discarded clothes from the floor, tidy rooms left in chaos, visit many shops in order to save centimos, and cook meals for those who consider them to be very ordinary. But, being a woman, I have no reason to complain.'

'You don't understand. When one has a day in which things have gone wrong and one is blamed for being ridiculously imaginative yet the other person is even more so, one begins to think nothing can be right. When I said the meal would be ordinary, it was just my depression, not what I really thought. And I didn't say "very" ordinary.'

'Yes, you did,' Juan argued.

'You know that's not true.'

'It is.'

'Your uncle,' Dolores said, 'has a reason for arguing.'

'What reason am I supposed to have?' Alvarez demanded.

'To avoid admitting that since you've started eating out, you do find my meals very ordinary.'

'I'm trying to explain that when I said "ordinary", I didn't mean they were ordinary.'

'You could not remember "inedible"?'

'It was simply that because of the delay, by your standards of perfection, the meal would not be as wonderful as it would have been.'

'As my mother used to say, a man's praise is as valuable as an empty purse.' She returned to the kitchen.

Alvarez spoke to Juan. 'Why did you tell your mother I said "very" when I didn't?'

Juan giggled.

Eva opened the front door of Aquila. Alvarez wished her a good morning.

'The señorita is not here; Pablo's driven her into Palma. She wanted to buy something.'

'And Luisa?'

'She's in the kitchen.'

'Then I can have a word with her and with you.'

'Why me?'

He smiled. 'No need to worry. You're not being blamed for anything.'

He stepped inside. After a moment, he suggested they went into the sitting room. She was reluctant to sit because she was afraid the señorita would return and think she was making herself far too much at home. He persuaded her that, if necessary, he would explain and no blame would be levelled at her.

He asked if she smoked. She didn't and in any case, the señor did not like smoking in the house and he . . . She stopped. 'I was talking stupid because the señor . . . He's . . .'

'You are not being stupid. It takes time to be at ease with the past. Tell me about him.'

'How d'you mean?'

'I want to know if there was anyone on bad terms with him. Someone who had had a row with him.'

The door opened and to her evident relief, Luisa entered, not Mary. 'More trouble?' Luisa asked.

'I'm just here to learn about the señor's life,' Alvarez answered. 'Whether he had had rows with anyone. The point is, I'm trying to find out if there was someone who had cause, or thought he had, to kill him.'

'Then I'd best take things off the cooker. Won't do them any harm to rest awhile.'

'I'm glad I'm not ruining a banquet.'

'If there was any fear of that, you wouldn't interrupt me.'

She left the room, soon returned and sat without hesitation. 'You're asking if someone didn't like the señor. He was a good man for a foreigner. Friendly. Always wanted to know if we were well. I had a pain in the leg and he said I was to see a specialist and he'd pay for that because it would take time before I could see someone on the national health.'

'Have you known him to have a row with anyone?'

'I can only think of Benito Muritano.'

'Tell me about him.'

'He lost his job when the small family painting firm closed down because of the bad times. He knows Juanito Santos and asked if the señor might want some painting done. Juanito spoke to the señor who said the house needed painting on the outside, so Benito could do that. The estimate said two coats of paint. When Benito, and the man who helped him, had finished the first coat, he said the job was done. The señor pointed out that the estimate was for two coats. Benito said one coat was the brush going up and the second coat was the brush coming down.'

'I've not heard that one before.'

'Benito didn't realize the señor was not just some ignorant foreigner and was surprised when he said what he thought of the fraud. Like any guilty man, Benito became angry at being caught out and threatened the señor. The señor paid half the estimate for a job half done and said if there was any trouble, he'd inform the police.'

'Has there been more trouble from him?'

'Never heard there was.'

'Have there been any other rows?'

'Depends what you mean. There was the guest who upset Eva.'

He turned to Eva. 'What happened?'

'It wasn't my fault. I didn't do anything to make him think I was that kind of a girl.' Eva spoke quickly.

'He was a fool to think you could be. He was a guest?'

'At one of the big parties.'

'Which gave enough work for six more staff,' Luisa said. 'We'd be clearing up long after it finished.'

'What did this man do?' Alvarez asked.

'I was leaving the breakfast room which was where we kept the extra food and all the drink. He comes in, fuffy, and nearly knocked me over . . . and started feeling me, put his hand up my skirt. I shouted and people came in. The señor spoke to the man in English; don't know what he said, but I'd never heard him near so angry before. He told Pablo to see the man left immediately.'

'Do you know his name?'

'No.'

He asked Luisa: 'Do you?'

'Hardly know the names of anyone he had to parties; not like them what came to meals. But the señor likely mentioned the name to the señorita and she might tell you who he was.'

'The señor was very close to her, wasn't he?'

'More like a father than an uncle. When she first came here, scared to do anything or to go anywhere, he couldn't have been kinder.'

'Does she have a boyfriend who can give her the comfort she needs?'

'There's been plenty of men her age invited, but there's none come back to ask her out.'

'Bad luck for her.'

'If you ask me, she didn't find it easy to be with any of 'em.'

'Well, that's the end of the inquisition! You've both been kind and helpful.' He stood.

'Find who did it,' Luisa said. 'The bastard should be made to pay for it.'

'He will.'
He left.

Normally, speaking to Salas was like stubbing a big toe.
But on this occasion, there would be no trouble and, perhaps,
even reluctant praise.

'It is Inspector Alvarez speaking, señorita. I should like
to speak to the superior chief.'

'He is busy.'

'This is important.'

'Then wait.'

He leaned back in the chair. The minutes passed.

'Yes?' said Salas impatiently.

'It is Inspector . . .'

 'What is it?'

'I have been speaking to the staff at Aquila, señor. You
remember you considered the motives for murder I put
forward were fanciful?'

'I imagine I used a stronger word.'

'I have to say I don't think they were any more fanciful
than the one you proposed. I have learned Señorita Farren
does not have, and has not had, a boyfriend, so there was
no one of whom the señor disapproved and because of
whom, he would have threatened to disinherit her. As I
mentioned at the time . . .'

'You lack the ability to understand if there is the possibility of a motive, that must be checked.'

'Which is what I did when I spoke to the Phillipses, but
you . . .'

'It is to be regretted you are incapable of differentiating
between feasible and ridiculous. Have you questioned the
staff?'

'Yes, señor.'

'And have you questioned Señor Kiernan about his IOU?'

'I intend to do that very soon.'

'Do you know where he lives?'

'No, but I will soon find out.'

'Have you learned who Miranda Pearson is?'

'Señor, I have been so busy . . .'

'Whatever has captured your enthusiasm, it clearly has not been work.'

'I have learned there are two more possible suspects to be considered.'

'They are?'

'Benito, a professional painter who was out of work. Being a friend of Santos, he asked if Señor Gill would give him a job. Señor Gill said he wanted the house painted outside with two coats. Only one coat was given. When questioned, Muritano claimed there had been one coat when the brush went up, a second when the brush came down.'

'The inhabitants of this island would find a way of defrauding a pauper. Señor Gill reported him for attempted fraud?'

'The señor paid half the agreed amount.'

'Then he was a fool.'

'It avoided Santos feeling dishonoured since he had recommended Muritano. Before he left with half the money he had hoped to gain, Benito threatened Señor Gill.'

'In what terms?'

'That is not known.'

'You haven't questioned him?'

'Señor, if I were two persons . . .'

'An unwelcome proposition. You will establish the facts. Who is the second person to whom you referred?'

'The señor gave large parties and at one of these, Eva, the maid, was accosted by a drunken Englishman who tried to molest her by . . .'

'You will not gain pleasure by detailing the nature of the molestation.'

'Señor Gill ordered Parra to see the man out of the house immediately. Since this was in the sight or hearing of other guests, his assault will have been widely known and he would have understood the contempt that would bring him.'

'What is his name?'

'The staff cannot identify him. It is possible the señorita will be able to do so, but she had driven in to Palma and was not at home when I was there.'

'You will speak to her the moment she returns. You will

identify and question, Muritano and Miranda Pearson. That done, you will be in a position to present a more valid report than you have just done. Whether in fact you do, is open to doubt.'

Alvarez replaced the receiver. He wondered how he could have stupidly thought he might receive even muted praise for his work.

TWELVE

Alvarez looked through the open window at the sunshine-covered walls on the other side of the narrow road. After fourteen phone calls, to fourteen Pearsons, he had learned nothing. None of those to whom he had spoken had known Robin Gill, and only one had heard of him.

Did Miranda live on the island? Mary had suggested she probably did. Was she not on the phone and therefore not listed in the directory? Yet now that it was easier to be connected, provided one didn't live in the back of beyond . . . He was thinking as he would have done years before. Mobiles allowed almost everyone to be on line. He had to call the communications centre and ask them to name the Pearsons they had on their lists.

The speaker at the communications centre was well trained. They were too busy at the moment, their computer had crashed, the law of privacy had to be respected, if he rang another day . . . Persistence and some rudeness gained the unwelcome news that no Pearson was listed as feminine. He would have to make further phone calls. But not when he was exhausted.

There was time before he could return home for lunch. So did he question Muritano? All that was known about him was, he had worked for a firm which had closed. But he was a friend of Santos.

Santos was on the far side of the fencing on Barca, making Alvarez wonder how any man could hold his life so cheaply. 'What's up?'

'I'm planting a vineyard,' Santos replied as, kneeling, he very carefully removed several newly surfaced weeds around Ophrys balerica.

'You're continuing to fuss over that thing? If it was mine . . .'

'It would be long since dead since you wouldn't come within a dozen metres of it. What are you after this time?' He stood.

'To ask where you were on Friday the fourth?'

'In Madrid, having grub at the Ritz.'

'Don't get too smart or I'll have you in on suspicion.'

'No sense of fun? I was here, of course.'

'Until when?'

'Twelve.'

'You didn't leave early?'

Santos hesitated. 'Maybe I was away a little quick. The old woman wasn't too fit.'

'No doubt she'd recovered and had cooked your lunch by the time you arrived back?'

He crossed to the fencing and climbed over it.

'Then you weren't here when the señor filmed or examined his beloved plant?'

'Are you going to ask all the same old questions?'

'I can't remember what your answers were.'

'Doubt you can give your own name without being reminded.'

'Will your wife corroborate the time you returned that day?'

'Why not ask her?'

'I will.'

'Then I'll tell her to help you up the front steps into the house. They're a bit high and could upset you.'

'You're so smart I'm beginning to think you didn't go home to lunch that day, but were here when the señor looked at his plant and you helped him over the side because he'd left you a little something in his will.'

'You're breeding more feathers between your ears by the minute.'

'There's no knowing what the friend of a fraudster will do.'

'You . . .' The Mallorquin was brief, but obscene.

'Then Benito Muritano isn't a friend of yours?'

'Not since he made me look as twisted as him.'

'I want a word with him.'

'About that painting job?'

'He must have been furious when his attempted fraud was exposed and he was paid half the estimate.'

'I suppose now you're going to suggest he got his own back? By pushing the señor over the edge. Ever seen a chicken attack a Giant Schnauzer? He's good for swindling, that's all.'

'I have to check him out.'

'My word's not good enough? You lot wouldn't believe a saint.'

'Since I'm not a saint yet, that's all right by me. Where does he live?'

'The village.'

'You expect me to call at each house to find out which one?'

'Wouldn't do you any harm around the belly. Sixteen, Carrer Loreto. And tell him that after dropping me in the pozo negro with the señor, I hope he ends up inside.'

Alvarez thankfully turned his back on the edge of the cliff. He crossed to the house. Luisa opened the door.

'If you want the señorita, Inspector, Pablo's just taken her into Llueso. He drives her because he says it's better until she's over the death of the señor. Always ready to help. He's a good husband.'

'There aren't many of those around these days. I'll return some other time.'

'She'll be glad to see you. Told me yesterday how much you've helped her.'

He was glad his help was appreciated.

Carrer Loreto was one-way. Alvarez passed the no-entry sign to face an oncoming car. He braked heavily and contemptuously ignored the other motorist's obvious signs of anger as he eased his way past; probably a foreigner who did not understand the local form of driving. He came to a halt in front of number sixteen. Like all other houses in the short road, it was stone built and dated from the nineteenth century.

He left the car, stepped into the entrada, and was

unsurprised to find a degree of comfort that contradicted the impression of bleakness the outer stone wall gave. He called out.

'Who is it?'

'Inspector Alvarez, cuerpo.'

'Wait.'

He waited.

When Muritano's wife finally came downstairs, he guessed she had been brightening her appearance.

'What's the trouble?' she uneasily asked.

'I need a word with your husband.'

'What's Benito been up to?'

'Nothing to cause any worry. Do you know where he is right now?'

'Working. Is it trouble with the Susana woman?'

'Not as far as I know. Where is he working?'

'Down in the port. Place that's been bought by a foreigner who wants it decorated from top to bottom.'

'Can you give me the address?'

'You say I don't need to worry, but what's your interest?'

'To ask him about some painting he's done.'

'Someone complaining? Can't see why it should bother you.'

He ignored the unasked question. 'Which house in the port?'

'Back of the school somewhere. Called Ca'n Felix.'

He thanked her and left.

Having driven down to the port, it took him fifteen frustrating minutes to find the modern bungalow in the centre of a small, slightly downmarket urbanizacíon.

Muritano was short, stocky, unshaven, and aggressive. 'So what d'you want?' he demanded, as they stood in the empty room, the walls of which were half-changed from an ugly blue to light green. From next door came the sounds of another painter at work.

'How many coats of paint make two?'

'What you getting at?'

'You are a friend of Juanito Santos.'

'I was until he behaved like a stupid sod.'

'He recommended you to Señor Gill to paint the outside of Aquila.'

'So?'

'The contract called for two coats.'

'Which is what the house got.'

'Because he was a foreigner, you reckoned he could be taken for a fool. You said it was one coat taking the roller up and one coat bringing it down again.'

'So what's wrong with that?'

'You want to make me laugh?'

'Don't look as if you know how.'

'I've talked to an honest painter. Two coats means two coats applied at different times.'

'Depends how you work.'

'You know the señor's dead?'

'I can read.'

'He was a foreigner, but he wasn't stupid. He understood you were trying to swindle him, so paid you only half the agreed sum.'

'Then he paid for the work done, and you can't charge me with anything.'

'How about murdering the señor?'

'Are you crazy?' he shouted.

Another man in paint-splattered overalls hurried into the room. 'Something up, Benito?'

'He's calling me a murderer.'

The newcomer spoke to Alvarez. 'Best stop causing trouble and move out quick or we'll help you out a lot quicker.'

'Inspector Alvarez, Cuerpo General de Policia.'

'You. It sounded like . . . I'd best get on with the work.' He hurriedly left.

Alvarez spoke to Muritano. 'Señor Gill expressed his opinion of you and your manner of working. You became very angry.'

'What d'you expect when he called me a thief. I ain't never stolen anything.'

'So angry that you determined to get your own back; after all, he'd turned the tables and made you look the fool.

You went up to Aquila to bluff or bully him into paying the rest of the money. He refused, probably commenting again on your dishonesty. Then he went to the end of Barca to look at the special orchid growing there. You were in such a hell of a rage that, seeing him so close to the edge of the rock, you rushed forward, belted him in the stomach, and forced him over the edge.'

'You . . . you're crazy,' he said again, now with fear, not anger.

'Where were you at thirteen hundred hours on Friday the fourth?'

'Working.'

'Where?'

Nervous panic caused confusion. 'I can't . . . can't say.'

'Unable to think up a feasible lie quickly enough?'

He shouted, 'Lorenzo!'

Lorenzo hurried in to the room. 'What now?'

'Where were we working on the fourth, Friday?'

'Wasn't here.'

'For Christ's sake, if you can't remember, he's going to arrest me.'

'Reckon we were doing that apartment down at the port.'

'You're right! That's where. Inspector, I was there.'

'And drove back for lunch, decided on the way to tell Señor Gill what you thought of him.'

'We don't go anywhere; we have lunch on the job to save time.'

'Who was with you on that job?'

'There was Lorenzo and someone else.'

'Who?'

Muritano began to speak, stopped, looked helpless.

Alvarez turned to Lorenzo. 'You were with him?'

'He's just said.'

'You'll swear to that on oath.'

'You're saying it'll be in court?'

'Could be, unless . . . Who was the other man?'

'Adolfo.'

'Why won't you believe me?' Muritano asked desperately.

'Because it's difficult to do so when you think one coat of paint is two coats.'

Adolfo's mother said he wasn't working that day, resentfully added that he was likely spending all his money at a bar or on a woman and would soon be trying to borrow from her until the next pay day.

'Does he have a favourite bar?'

She named a couple she knew he frequently visited. He was not at the first one; at the second, a waiter identified Adolfo, sitting at an outside table with a woman.

Glass in hand – it was only fair to offer custom when information had been given – Alvarez went out on to the pavement and over to the table at which a young man with long hair drawn into a ponytail was seated opposite a woman who lacked discretion in make-up and clothing.

'Adolfo?'

He looked up and stared at Alvarez with contemptuous indifference.

'I'd like a word.'

Adolfo picked up his glass and emptied it. He spoke to his companion. 'Ready for another?'

'Don't think I should.'

'That's the time to have it.'

She giggled.

Alvarez asked, 'Where were you at thirteen hundred hours on Friday the fourth?'

'Sod off, old man.'

Alvarez's annoyance was immediate. He could no longer claim to be a young man, but he certainly wasn't an old one. 'Cuerpo.'

'What . . . Why . . .?'

'Been wondering if you've been peddling drugs and robbing tourists or dealing in smuggled booze and fags.'

The woman stood. 'I've got to rush.'

'Hang on. He's talking horse shit.'

She hurried away.

Alvarez settled on the seat she had vacated.

Adolfo no longer spoke belligerently. 'Look, I've never touched crack or—'

'Where were you?'

'What . . . what day did you say?'

'Friday the fourth.'

'I swear I wasn't doing any of what you said.'

'D'you sometimes work as a casual, doing painting?'

'Yes, but—'

'For whom?'

He named four men, the third of whom was Muritano.

'When and where did you last work for him?'

'A short time back, doing some apartments down along the front.'

'What was the work routine?'

'He gave us the paint, brushes, and rollers . . .'

'Where did you have lunch that day?'

'In the apartment we was working in. Always the same with him. Sandwiches and a drink and he's shouting back to work. A bloody slave-driver . . .'

Before he left, Alvarez was tempted to tell Alfonso to be a man and have a haircut.

Alvarez picked a banana out of the earthenware bowl in the centre of the dining-room table. 'I've had a frustrating time, working hard and getting nowhere.'

'Her boyfriend turned up?' Jaime suggested.

'Why would that upset uncle?'Juan asked.

'Your father,' Dolores said, 'has a nonsensical tongue after many glasses of wine. You and Isabel have finished your meals, so you can leave.'

'I want to stay.'

'You will need to be very much older before you can do as you wish, regardless of other people.'

The children left.

Alvarez peeled the banana. 'Hours on the telephone, speaking to hundreds of people, and not one of them the person I want.'

'Who are you trying to get hold of?' Dolores asked.

'Any young female who can't run faster than him,' Jaime said.

She sighed.

'Miranda Pearson,' Alvarez answered.

'Why can't you look her up in the directory?' Jaime asked.

'What do you think I've been doing?'

'No knowing where you're concerned.'

'I've tried all the Pearsons in the book and with mobiles.'

'Maybe she doesn't live on the island any longer; maybe, she doesn't really exist.'

'A non-existent isn't left ten thousand pounds in a will.'

'Ten thousand! No wonder you're in a hurry. Find her before anyone else and you've the chance of a share.'

'Is she married?' Dolores asked.

'Almost certainly.'

'Then you may have her maiden name.'

'And the will was made before she married? Takes a genius to think of that,' he said admiringly.

'You must think we've nothing to do all day,' the under-director at the records office said.

He did. But he needed their goodwill. 'I've been told you're having to work harder than ever with the alteration in the form of residencias.'

'And does anyone thank us for all the overtime we have to do?'

'Not if it's like our outfit. Not a moment for a chat and work twenty-four hours a day and you're told you should work longer.'

'If some of us don't break down from stress, it'll be a miracle.'

'Get a doctor to say you must have a break.'

'They won't play until one's a hospital case.'

'But if one of them has a cold, it's an emergency?'

'Them and us. The whole outfit is them and us. When my decimo comes up, I'll be out of this office like I was running the hundred metres.'

'And when mine does, I'll buy fifty hectares of land and grow . . .'

'Dreams. Keep a man willing to live . . . Did you say you wanted something?'

'Have you done as I ordered?' Salas asked at 1700 hours.

'It has all been very difficult,' Alvarez answered.

'Is there any task simple enough not to cause you trouble?'

'I tried to identify Miranda Pearson, who is the legatee in Señor Gill's will and has been left . . .'

'Try to accept that I am conversant with the facts.'

'I understood you always wanted to be told what and whom a report concerns before that report is made.'

'It escapes you that such order only concerns reports which require identification?'

'I don't think I understand the difference.'

'I lack sufficient time to explain in simple terms. Have you made any progress?'

'I phoned dozens, perhaps hundreds of Pearsons listed in the directory. None of them knew, or had met, Señor Gill. I asked mobile to give me a list of all the Pearsons on their books. The result was similar.'

'You have failed your task? Not unusual.'

'I realized the will might have been written before she was married and Señor Gill had not known her name had changed, or had not thought to alter his will.'

'A probability which should have occurred to you far sooner.'

'I asked records to carry out a search of maiden names since a foreign woman has to give that when applying for a residencia.'

'Are you about to inform me that a week has seven days and there are sixty minutes in an hour?'

'Why would I do that?'

'Because you seem determined to waste my time by informing me of facts of which I am fully cognisant.'

'Señor and Señora Morton-Smith live in Raix. Her maiden name was Pearson, Miranda Harriet Pearson. So I will speak to her as soon as possible.'

'Which is immediately. You do not think it necessary to tell me where Raix is?'

'I thought you would know, so did not wish to waste your time.'

'It is difficult to decide whether you lack any common sense or are once more trying to be insolent.'

There was a pause.

'One thing is significant,' Alvarez said.

'What?'

'That she is married.'

'Since marriage is a normal occurrence amongst reputable people, the significance escapes me.'

'Señor Gill's bequest has to suggest, as I pointed out previously, there was adultery.'

'Only to someone who relentlessly seeks immorality.'

'I will question her to learn what was the relationship between her, her husband, and Señor Gill.'

'Are you now suggesting there was a very close relationship.'

'A ménage à trois? I rather doubt that. I'm surprised, señor, you should refer to such an event.'

'I was doing no such thing. Only a disturbed mind could presume I was.'

'What I meant was, whether the husband had any suspicion of his wife's affair.'

'One day, you might learn to say what you mean. You will interview her this evening and report to me tomorrow morning.'

'But . . .'

'You are about to tell me she has flown to India?'

'It is already seven thirty.'

'Time is of no account to those who wish to carry out their tasks efficiently.'

'It will take well over an hour to get there because one has to drive slowly over the mountains and the road often has no guard and there can be a fall of ten, twenty metres . . .'

'You are still unable to control your irrational fears? You will go there in the early morning and report to me the moment you return.'

'Yes, señor.'

If he arrived too early, he would interrupt their breakfast.

Relatively few tourists drove from Llueso to Laraix and along the Tremontana. What the many missed were the bleak, often dramatic mountains, weathered and striated by wind and rain, occasional narrow valleys which were once farmed but now were abandoned by those no longer willing to accept such harsh surroundings, and the wildlife – amongst which, the prince was the black vulture, the king, the golden eagle.

Alvarez reached the Laraix monastery, founded to honour the small figure of the Virgin Mary which had been observed when a miraculous light had been seen under a bush. After so nerve-racking a drive, he needed to relax and a coñac at one of the cafés helped him. Fifteen minutes slid by before he drove past the monastery and continued up to Raix.

The bungalow was at the highest point of the small village and provided a dramatic view of the mountains which both humbled a man and enhanced their majesty. Three concrete steps gave access to a rising path of stone chippings which bisected a garden in which some of the plants seen at sea level could not be grown because of winter cold and snow. He knocked on the front door. It was opened by a slightly younger man than he, who held keys in his right hand. 'What do you want?' he asked in mangled Spanish as he looked at his watch.

'Señor Morton-Smith?'

'Yes?'

'Inspector Alvarez of the Cuerpo General de Policia.'

He began to speak in poor Spanish but stuttered to a halt.

'Would you like to speak English, señor?' Alvarez said in that language.

'Thank God for that! Is something wrong?'

'I am here merely to ask a few questions.'

'I'm in one hell of a rush; late already to get to the airport and pick up friends. Could I possibly see you when I get back?'

'Is your wife here?'

'Yes.'

'Then I need not detain you. She can probably tell me what I need to know. And if she can't, I will speak to you another time.'

'That's jolly kind. Do come in.'

As he entered, Alvarez reflected that luck was with him. He could question her without her husband's being present. A short passage gave access to the sitting room which was large, probably at the expense of other rooms. Picture windows offered the same sweeping view he had enjoyed when by the car.

'Miranda, this is Inspector Alvarez. He speaks perfect English and wants to know something, but has kindly said I can continue on to the airport. If you can't answer his questions, he'll come back another time.'

She said hullo to him, and he replied.

'I'll be off, then,' Morton-Smith said hurriedly. 'Again, many thanks, Inspector.' He left in a rush.

'Please sit,' she said.

She was in early middle age, attractive but certainly not beautiful. Light-brown hair, round face with dark-brown eyes, a pleasant mouth, a graceful neck.

'May I offer you a drink, Inspector?'

'That would be very welcome. We call this the thirsty month.'

'With reason. What would you like?'

'A coñac with just ice, if I may.'

He watched her leave. Not a woman he would have expected to cuckold her husband. But then women were masters of deception.

She returned, handed him a glass and sat. 'Your health.'

'And yours, señora.' He drank.

'How may I be able to help you?'

'I am glad you are on your own, señora.'

'Why?'

'I have to ask you about a matter that is very personal.'

'Then it's me you want to speak to, not Alex?'

'That is correct.'

'Why should you be glad I'm on my own?'

'Have you learned that Señor Gill, who lived near Llueso, very unfortunately recently died in a fall?'

'Oh, my God!' She stared through the window.

'You knew him?'

It was a time before she answered. 'Yes.'

'Very well?'

'No, I can't say that; not recently, anyway. Unfortunately, he and Alex never got on well together, so after we moved here, we only saw him occasionally.'

'Was there any reason for this lack of friendship?'

'Just a case of two people who are polite to each other, but have no wish to become genuinely friendly. Ask them why and they probably couldn't answer.'

'Your husband may not have said so, but was he worried about your past friendship with Señor Gill?'

'Good heavens, no. It was a case of "I do not like thee, Doctor Fell", and not "I hate thee Doctor Fell".'

'Might he not have been worried about the degree of that friendship?'

'Inspector, I'm sorry, but I don't know what you're getting at.'

'Señor Gill has left you a legacy of ten thousand pounds in his will.'

'Poor Robin,' was her delayed reaction.

'Yet none of his staff could tell me who you were.'

'Hardly surprising since we saw Robin so seldom and when we did, we had lunch in a restaurant. The only time we went to his house was for a large party and his staff wouldn't have known who we were.'

'Can you suggest why he left you a legacy?'

'Friendship.'

'It could be said to be unusual for friendship to be so generously rewarded.'

'What an odd and rather nasty thing to say!' She waited for him to comment, but he remained silent. 'You're not . . . You don't think I might have had an affair with him?'

'Yes, señora.'

'I'll be damned! You see me clothed in scarlet?'

'It is not true?'

'Couldn't be further from the truth. I'm a boring, old-fashioned wife who likes to remain faithful to her husband.'

'Señor Gill did not get on with your husband, you did not see him often, yet he left you several thousands of pounds.'

'You don't believe me when I tell you we had no affair?'

'My job demands I believe no one unless I have good reason to do so.'

'That must make your life difficult and miserable.'

'It certainly does not make for cheerfulness, señora.'

'I will try to lighten your misery. My father and Robin were great friends. Robin was an inventor and thought up something in the early electronic days which he was convinced would be very successful. He hadn't much money, so he asked the bank to fund him, but they weren't convinced and refused. My father offered Robin his savings to go ahead. Robin was highly successful and soon repaid the debt. He never forgot my father's kindness and I imagine this legacy is because of that. You say you're conditioned to disbelieve me, so you'd better read the letter he wrote to my father when he repaid the money and which I've kept for sentimental reasons.'

He stood. 'Señora, having insulted you once, I will not do so again by asking to read the letter.'

He left.

Alvarez picked up the receiver, paused, replaced it. Surely there had to be some way in which to avoid the unavoidable?

There was not. He lifted it again and this time dialled.

'Yes?' said Angela Torres.

'It is Inspector Alvarez speaking . . .'

'Wait.'

He picked up a pencil and drew a childlike picture of Salas with two devil's horns on his elongated head.

'It is now well into the morning,' Salas said. 'Were you not instructed to phone me the moment you returned to the office?'

'It took time . . .'

'I am uninterested in mindless excuses. Are you going to make a report or is there nothing to say because you omitted to carry out your orders?'

'I drove to the home of the Morton-Smiths and . . .'

'Who?'

'Miranda, the wife, was Miranda Pearson before marriage. As I arrived, he was leaving . . .'

'Who was?'

'The husband.'

'Then say so.'

'That was very fortunate.'

'Why?'

'It meant she . . . Señora Morton-Smith was on her own.'

'She confessed to her adultery?'

'No, because . . .'

'Of your incompetent questioning.'

'Because the reason for the legacy was not what it had seemed to be.'

'Appeared to you to be.'

'Her father had helped Señor Gill financially in the past and the legacy was a further expression of his thanks to, and regard for, her father.'

'To be certain I am hearing what you believe you are saying, do you no longer believe this legacy to be a consequence of the wife's adultery with Señor Gill?'

'That is so.'

'Señor Morton-Smith had no motive for murdering Señor Gill?'

'It seems not.'

'Then another of your proposed motives is exposed as nonsense.'

'It did seem obvious . . .'

'Only to an obsessed mind.'

'That's not just.'

'Only because it does not mention obtuse and impercipient.'

The line was dead.

THIRTEEN

Luisa opened the front door of Aquila. 'Good morning, Inspector,' she said cheerfully.

'And to you. Is Parra not here?'

'He has driven into the village to buy some stores. Will you come through? The señorita will be very glad to see you.'

He followed her, unkindly decided she had put on a little weight since he had first met her unless her dress was too tight for someone with her posterior dimensions. She and Pablo made an unlikely couple, but then in another's eyes, many couples were strangely matched. One saw beauty, warmth, trustworthiness; another, plainness, egotism, unreliability. But for this, would there be marriages?

Mary smiled as he followed Luisa into the sitting room, cooled by the air-conditioning unit. 'I'm sorry I was out the last time you were here.'

'It's given me the chance to come here this morning.'

'Would you like coffee, señorita?' Luisa asked.

Mary looked at Alvarez. 'For you?'

'Yes, please.'

Luisa left.

'Is this business or pleasure?' Mary asked.

'Ninety-five per cent pleasure, five per cent questioning.'

'There can still be some you haven't asked?'

'They grow like viruses.'

'And are often as nasty. Is the sun worrying you? If so, lower the awning.'

'It's fine, thanks. Makes the room cheerful.'

'But when the sky's all cloud, the mountains become dark, the island sulks . . . Enrique, would you help a maiden in distress?'

'Of course. What's wrong?'

'Something silly. I dreamt Robin and I were picnicking

and when I awoke . . . I've been feeling lost. As you walked in here, I wondered if you'd take me down to the bay again?'

'Naturally.'

'"A verray parfit gentil knight". Ask the questions quickly so they're over and done with.'

'I don't know how long ago it was, but at one of your parties, there was trouble with a guest. Can you remember that?'

'I'm not certain what "trouble" means. When a number of expats get together, there are often hiccups. Someone plays the fool and lands in the pool, drinks too much, helps himself to a bottle of champagne to take home or is rude because he's so superior – wives of retired high-ranking servicemen are past masters at that.'

'A guest was objectionable to Eva.'

'Him! When Robin learned about that, he was furious. It wasn't just Frank's appalling behaviour. Robin knew I'd be upset because it would make me remember. He ordered Frank out of the house and told Pablo to make certain he went.'

'He must have felt humiliated?'

'Angry because he claimed Robin was making a scene out of nothing. For Frank, wealth equals superiority, so maids are for the taking. Why d'you want to know about this?'

'He must have believed he had reason to hate your uncle.'

'I suppose . . . Enrique are you thinking . . .' She stopped.

'I'd just like a word with him. What's his surname?'

'Foster.'

'Where does he live?'

'On the outskirts of the port in a large house with every possible accessory – sauna, indoor pool as well as an outdoor one, gymnasium. It's called Ca'n Foster, naturally.'

'Is he married?'

'To Agatha. A grande dame. Or so she believes. Leaves the island in the summer because the sun isn't good for her complexion. If she had one left, one could understand her complaint.'

'Does he remain here?'

'Mostly. Probably by choice.'

'I'll call and have a word with him, but from the sound of things, not by choice.'

'When?'

'This afternoon. Right now, a rescue drive down to the port takes priority.'

Ca'n Foster was a large and lumpy house, the garden was large with water-thirsty lawn and flower beds, the outdoor pool was large, and the Bentley in the garage was large.

The front door was opened by a middle-aged man, dressed with the formality of an upper servant.

'Is Señor Foster here?' Alvarez asked.

'You are?'

'Inspector Alvarez, Cuerpo General de Policia.'

The man's surprise was momentarily visible. 'Will you come in, please, and I will ask if Señor Foster is free.'

The hall was large, the colourful carpet on the marble floor was large, the two vases, filled with flowers, were large, and the paintings of hunting scenes in England which hung on one wall were large.

'Would you wait here, Inspector.'

Alvarez studied the paintings and tried to make sense of the English pleasure in risking death on horseback.

Foster entered the hall from one of the adjoining rooms. He was just under two metres tall, lean, and his face had the features of a man who never doubted his own authority. 'What do you want?' He spoke in English – Spanish was for foreigners – with clipped tones.

'I should like to ask you some questions, señor.'

'Why?'

'I am investigating the death of Señor Gill and have reason to think you may be able to help me'

'You think incorrectly.'

'Nevertheless, I shall need to ask you certain things.'

'I suppose you'd better come in here.' He walked towards the nearest door and stopped. 'Perez.'

Perez, who had let Alvarez into the house, hurried into the hall.

'I'll have the usual.'

Foster opened the door and went into the room. Alvarez followed. 'The usual'? A drink? He would be asked what he would like; he could reasonably hope for one of the top brandies.

'I haven't time to waste, but you might as well sit.'

They sat.

'If you're investigating Gill's death, why come here?'

'I think you knew the señor?'

'We'd met.'

'You were not great friends?'

'No.'

'Was there a reason for that?'

'The good lady went to a lot of trouble trying to teach the niece how to behave in society – proper society, not the ragbag here. Gill told her not to interfere. One is not friendly with someone capable of such rudeness. We may meet in a shop, but both the good lady and I try to avoid doing so if possible.'

'Who is the good lady?'

'Who the devil do you think? My wife.'

'Is she here?'

'In England.'

The door opened and Perez entered with a silver salver on which was a filled flute. He held the salver out for Foster to take the glass, then left.

Alvarez was as surprised as outraged by the appalling manners of his not being offered a drink while Foster enjoyed champagne.

Foster put his glass down on a runner on the small table at his side. 'Do you intend to say why you're here?'

'I need to speak to all who knew Señor Gill in order to learn if there was the possibility someone had reason to wish him dead.'

'Then I am unable to assist you.'

'Have you ever been to a party at his house?'

'Once, since I did not realize the mixed nature of the event.'

'Was there trouble during that party?'

'Are you here because of that bloody stupid nonsense?'

'If you are referring to an incident concerning the maid, Eva, yes, I am. I believe Señor Gill ordered you out of his house and told the manservant to make certain you left immediately because you had molested his maid.'

'Quite incapable of understanding I could never behave in the manner he claimed.'

'Did you molest her?'

'Damn your insolent question!'

'More than one person has told me that you did.'

'Give me their names and I'll sue them for slander.'

'Would you like to tell me what did happen?'

'The waiting was so poor, I had to go into another room to refill my glass. The maid started to come out, holding a tray of canapés, didn't look where she was going and banged in to me. The tray went for a burton; I had to hold on to her to save myself falling. The next thing is, she starts screaming.'

'It was pure chance your hand ended up under her skirt?'

'That is a monstrous lie.'

'Eva claims you ran your hand up her leg.'

'An uneducated woman's fantasy.'

'She also says you fondled her body.'

'Perverted imagination.'

'You deny the allegations?'

'You imagine I would mess around with a maid?'

'Why not?'

'I doubt you are capable of understanding that a person in my position would never betray himself in such a manner.'

'Did you have a friend present who will confirm your account of events?'

'You are inferring I'm a bloody liar?'

'I have made no such inference, señor.'

'Haven't you just asked for corroboration?'

'That is necessary since at the moment, it is just your word against Eva's.'

'You'd give her evidence the same weight as mine?'

'Why not? You must have been very angry when you understood how people would be regarding you with amused contempt. You decided to return to Aquila and have a row with Señor Gill. When you arrived, he was, by chance, on his own. Mary was in Palma and the staff were away. Señor Gill was either studying or photographing the orchid of which he was so proud and therefore was beyond the fencing. What happened then? Did the opportunity to gain revenge on the man who had named you a lecherous bounder become too great to resist? You approached him, saying you were there to apologize, and pushed him over the edge?'

'Ignorant absurdity.'

'What is your friend's name and address?'

There was a long silence before Foster finally said: 'Harrison. Flat four, Neckham, Port Llueso.'

'One final question. Where were you around one in the afternoon on Friday the fourth?'

'Is that when he fell? I don't know where I was and I don't give a damn.'

Alvarez stood. 'It would be to your benefit to remember.' He went into the hall and approached the front door. Perez hurried past him to open it. 'A fruitful meeting, Inspector?'

Alvarez was in the car before he thought of a smart answer.

FOURTEEN

Neckham was a four-storey block which had replaced one of the old family homes along the pine walk. As he approached the building, Alvarez's annoyance increased. One more feature of the past had vanished in the name of profit. Years previously, the row of large, detached houses, each within its own grounds, luxurious by the standards of the day, had been owned by the grandees, mainly from Palma, who had occupied them during the summer and often at times of festivals. Now there were many fewer and those which remained had often been split into two or three flats.

Hot and slightly breathless from the walk, he turned into the small garden and continued into the lobby which was lined with lightly engraved glass. How much more attractive had been ancient wood and lime-washed walls. The name board by the post boxes set in the wall listed G. Harrison on the top floor. He crossed to the lift – one modernism of which he approved.

Under the switchboard was a button on its own, marked 'Penthouse'. He pressed this. Through a small grill, a man asked: 'Who is it?' Obviously, the hoi polloi were to be kept at bay. He gave his name.

The lift rose, stopped, and the door opened. A man was waiting in the long passage/hall. Tall, balding, he wore an open-neck shirt and linen shorts. On his right wrist was a gold Rolex.

'Señor Harrison?'

'Yes.'

'I apologize for troubling you, but I have some questions I'd like to ask.'

'No doubt, following your visit to Mr Foster?'

Perhaps Salas might have expected him to drive directly from Foster's house to Harrison's flat in order to prevent any collaboration between the two men. But since there would have been at least a twenty-minute gap whilst he was driving down to the port . . .

'Come on through after you've told me what you'd like to drink.'

Here was a man who understood that when in Mallorca, one did as the Mallorquins did. He asked for a brandy.

The sitting room was well furnished in modern style; through the picture window much of the bay was visible above the pine trees. Live there and one had no need to seek beauty.

He was standing by the window when Harrison returned with a glass in each hand. He passed one to Alvarez. 'Admiring the view?'

'As beautiful as anywhere in the world.'

'A true Lluesian!'

There was a sharp buzz in the hall.

'That'll be my wife, back from shopping. Please excuse me.' He went out.

Alvarez continued to stare at the bay as he drank. Wealth had brought this view of paradise along with the flat. Some sage of a parsimonious nature had said that wealth did not make for happiness. It certainly gave happiness a hefty leg up.

Harrison returned, carrying two shopping bags, along with his wife whose age was probably very similar to his, but whose appearance, through the skills of make-up and dieting, suggested she was several years less. 'Inspector Alvarez, Susan.'

'Hullo, Inspector,' she said with a smile. He returned her greeting. Her stylish appearance reminded him he had intended to change his shirt that morning.

'George says you're here because of that unfortunate episode at Aquila. So very unnecessary . . . I must go through to the kitchen and start to prepare lunch.' She took the bags from her husband and left.

At Harrison's suggestion, Alvarez settled on an easy chair.

'If you'll tell what you'd like to know, Inspector, I'll do my best to answer.'

'You were at the party given by Señor Gill at which there was an unfortunate incident?'

'I was, with my wife. It was very unfortunate that Robin made such a scene of it when he could have handled matters far more diplomatically.'

'Yet he must have been annoyed when a guest molested his maid.'

'He should have realized that simply wasn't possible. Frank won't object if I say that he wouldn't molest a maid if they were on their own and she was stark naked. It simply doesn't fit the picture he has of himself. He was a little squiffy which was why he tripped and grabbed hold of the maid for support.'

'Eva claims his hand went up inside her skirt.'

'Panicky imagination. I'll bet that unlike so many of her contemporaries, she is still constrained by the moral guidelines her mother laid down. Reputation is as valuable as virginity; lose either and any chance of a good marriage is lost. Maybe a hand did land on her buttock or breast as Frank tried to hold his balance, but that was unintentional.'

'You seem very certain of that.'

'I was close by when Frank started to come into the room as the maid was leaving with a tray of canapés. Frank tried to avoid her, stumbled, caught hold of her to prevent his falling, and the next second she was screaming.'

'Señor Gill thought it was far more serious.'

'Because he wasn't present and was too ready to accept her wild accusations.'

'Have you spoken to Señor Foster about that incident?'

'Naturally.'

'What did he say about it?'

'Cursed Robin in quarterdeck style for being so stupid.'

'Was Señor Foster very angry?'

'For a time. But then . . .'

'Yes?'

'He's a queer old bird. After a while he decided this cloud did have a silver lining.'

'What did he mean?'

'His wife declared she was humiliated by his behaviour, was not prepared to suffer the unspoken sneers of friends, was returning to England and didn't know if she'd return. He declared it as the most productive fumble he had never had.'

'He welcomed his wife leaving him?'

'You have not met her? A born spinster.'

'But he must surely have been disturbed by the knowledge many believed he had sexually assaulted a young lady?'

'Meeting him casually, you'd never think him the man who lurks behind the mask. Eventually, he found even that amusing. He thought some of the widows would start asking him for drinks.'

'He seemed far more concerned than that when I spoke to him earlier.'

'What would you expect? To be questioned by a policeman. So very infra dig.'

Alvarez looked at his watch. It was only seven minutes since he had last looked, yet he had judged it to be at least twenty. A brave man would not fear shadows. But he was not a brave man. Perhaps he should consider the evidence once more before making a report? Perhaps Salas had left the office to misplay a game of golf?

He phoned.

Of course the superior chief was in his office, working, Señorita Torres waspishly told him. 'Wait.'

The connection was made. 'Inspector Alvarez from Llueso speaking, señor.'

'Well?'

'I have been conducting further enquiries concerning the death of Señor Gill. I questioned Señor Foster who, as you will remember . . .'

'Then there is no need to waste my time telling me.'

'I asked him where he was at the time of Señor Gill's death. His reply was that he did not know and did not care. I found it difficult to judge whether those were the words of a man who couldn't be bothered to remember because he was innocent of Señor Gill's death or was intending to give such impression.

'I asked him about his alleged sexual assault of Eva.

He said he had automatically held on to her to prevent himself falling and had not touched any part of her to cause alarm.'

'What did that mean?'

'Her breast or her . . .'

'You will not continue.'

'At no time had he slipped his hand up her leg.'

'She was hardly likely to have made so embarrassing a claim unless she had good reason to do so.'

'Señor Foster thought it was wishful thinking.'

'Outrageous!'

'Understandable.'

'Your comment is as outrageous as his. No young woman would ever wish to suffer such attention.'

'I don't think one can be certain of that.'

'You can condone such behaviour?'

Alvarez hastily said: 'Señor Harrison confirms Señor Foster's evidence. Señor Foster was making his way into a second room as Eva was coming out of it. She banged into him or he tripped, instinctively held on to her in order not to fall. If his hands made contact of an undesirable nature, this would have been unintentional.

'One might not expect his innocence to lessen the anger he must be expected to have had for Señor Gill's behaviour. Being publicly ordered out of the house made it obvious that Eva's accusations were accepted as justified. However . . .'

'Yes?'

'It does seem Señor Foster was not as furious as one might imagine, considering the dead man so publicly ordered him out.'

'You are referring to Señor Gill, when he was alive?'

'Yes.'

'You have yet to understand the difference between a live and a dead man.'

'Señor Harrison suggested Señor Foster was originally furious, but eventually treated the incident as a beneficial one.'

'The alleged assault of a young woman can be beneficial? Their imagination is perverse.'

'It wasn't the assault, it was the allegation. His wife felt so humiliated that she returned to England.'

'Extraordinary.'

'Something else was said which seems to confirm Señor Foster was not burning with fury.'

'One does not burn unless there is a cause.'

'Señor Foster was wondering if some of the widowed ladies would be inviting him.'

'That is likely when they will believe he has behaved so disgracefully?'

'For one or two, it could well be a . . .' Alvarez stopped sharply.

'A what?'

'I've forgotten the word, señor. Perhaps the inference should be judged to be black humour.'

'What inference?'

'That the widows . . .'

'Can you never finish a sentence? Speaking to you is like trying to finish a jigsaw with missing pieces. Are you now saying that Señor Foster was regarding the episode almost lightly?'

'It does seem so.'

'You understand that if he was not extremely angry and his anger did not last, he will not have had reason to encompass Señor Gill's death?'

'That is logical.'

'Why is why you are so reluctant to accept the fact? You have repeatedly claimed to know the motive is to know there was murder. You have introduced motives which can only be described as the products of an incoherent imagination. As a result, a great deal of time has been completely wasted.'

'No, señor, not wasted. My work has reduced the number of suspects and I still have to question Señor Kiernan.'

'The last man you claim has a motive. Then according to you, he must be guilty. I expect this case to be completed within the next twenty-four hours.'

Alvarez replaced the receiver.

FIFTEEN

'I met Beatriz when I was shopping,' Dolores said, as she put a plateful of cut bread on the dining-room table.

As she returned to the kitchen, Alvarez and Jaime tried to guess what that remark portended. In turn, each shrugged his shoulders.

'She is obnoxiously inquisitive,' she called out.

'Show me the woman who isn't,' Jaime muttered.

'She wanted to know if Enrique is finally getting married.'

Alvarez had to ask: 'What did you tell her?'

'What would you expect me to say?'

Only the gods could answer that.

'I said such matters were not to do with me since you are my cousin, not my son. Do you know what she then said?'

They remained silent. Her tone had been indecipherable.

'She said you looked more like my father than a son.'

'Silly bitch!' Alvarez muttered.

She looked through the bead curtain. 'It was strange to receive a compliment from her. But, of course, I do look considerably younger than you, even though there are few years between us. However, I do not drink alcohol as if it were water.' She retired.

A woman's calendar ran backwards, Alvarez thought. There were only very few years between them. And when she had been cooking or tidying the house, was hot and flushed, she could be mistaken for his older sister.

Dolores called out: 'She remarked that the woman was considerably younger than you.'

Alvarez drank. Her reason for this conversation was clear.

'She was not a beauty, but who, at your age, could be choosy. When she'd finished, I said her tongue was too loose, you were doing a good deed and helping an

Englishwoman overcome the death of her uncle. That made Beatriz look stupid.' She looked through the curtain again. 'I trust that she was the woman who you were with? That it was not some foreigner half your age?'

'I was with Mary.'

'And it is simply your good nature which causes you to see her so often, to leave work and take her down to the beach?'

'What else?'

'Need a suggestion?' Jaime asked.

'You wish to say something you will consider amusing, but we will find juvenile and objectionable?' she asked.

'I was just going to say something pleasant.'

'Which was?'

He fiddled with his glass.

'You have forgotten? Or, for once, you have found the manners not to speak obscenely in front of me? Aiyee! A mouse tries to roar, but can only squeak.'

'Stupid female,' Alvarez muttered.

'Hang on.' Jaime spoke angrily. 'She may talk stupidly, but you don't insult my wife.'

'I was referring to Beatriz. Her saying I looked like Dolores' father.'

'Why get upset over that? She once told Dolores she's seen me eyeing a bit in a bikini in the old square.'

'Had you?'

'Can't remember. It would keep women quieter if they didn't have so much time to push their noses into other people's business. Of course, then they wouldn't have anything much to occupy themselves.'

Jaime had been speaking too loudly.

'Unless they are married,' she called out, 'when they are forever having to deal with their husbands' stupidity.'

Kiernan's flat faced inland and the only view was of the tops of mountains above other buildings. The rectangular sitting room was ill-proportioned and in order to watch the television, chairs had to be set out as in an old-fashioned railway carriage. The furnishings were Ikean.

Kiernan and his wife were in their late sixties. Within minutes, Alvarez had learned how for years they had longed for the sun, sea, and peace the island offered. Kiernan had retired, they had sold up in England and moved. For a while, life had matched their dreams. Then had come the financial crisis and the depreciation of the pound against the euro. The cost of living had risen sharply – electricity had doubled, or more, in price – and they had had to contemplate returning to England. They had very soon learned it would be difficult to sell their flat and the amount they gained would be insufficient to buy much of a house in England. Their son, with two children, didn't have room for them in his home . . .

Alvarez managed to bring a verbal end to their troubles when he said: 'This was why you borrowed money from Señor Gill?'

Kiernan had a high forehead and a beaky nose and astonishment disarranged his features so that his face became gnome-like. 'How . . . How do you know we did?'

His wife reached over and gripped his hand.

'I found your IOU amongst the señor's papers. Officials will want to know if you accept the debt.'

'You said you're a detective. So why are you asking about that?' Her face was heavily lined, her complexion poor and childbearing had left her dumpy. Time had not been kind to her.

'Steady on, Nell,' Kiernan said.

'I'm sure there's something more to the question than there seems to be.'

She had a sharp mind, Alvarez noted. 'The amount of the IOU is for ten thousand pounds. Did you receive that money from Señor Gill?'

She answered, making it clear she usually fought their battles. 'We were having trouble meeting the mortgage repayments on this flat which was why he lent us the money.'

'When was this, señora?'

Her rate of speaking quickened. 'We were in trouble. Without enough money to continue living here, it had become a nightmare.'

He hated his job when it exposed the misery of others.

Kiernan spoke bitterly. 'It reached the point where it seemed the only thing to do was walk into the sea and drown.'

'And I told him, I'd rather we had to live in a debtors' prison than be without each other,' she said fiercely. 'Robin met me in the village and said I looked terrible and was there anything he could do to help. I . . . I tried to control myself, but couldn't when he asked what was making me so miserable. I couldn't stop myself, even though he'd think I was asking him for money because he was rich. He listened, said life could be easier for us if we had no mortgage and could repay capital when we were in a position to do so, asked how much was owing, said he'd lend it to us. When I returned here, I was so excited as I told Tim, but he . . .'

'Being a bloody fool,' Kiernan said, 'I was more concerned with the humiliation of borrowing money than with the tremendous mental relief he was offering Nell.'

She continued. 'It took ages to persuade Tim that it really wouldn't be all that different from borrowing from a bank.'

'Because it was nothing of the sort. Robin was a friend. In the end, I agreed we'd borrow from him, provided we could repay regularly, and said I'd get a notario to draw up whatever papers he thought necessary. He told me there was no need to make a notario richer than he already was, I could give him a simple IOU.

'The first time I repaid him, I asked him what interest I was to add. He was hurt that I should expect him to ask for any interest.'

'How much did you repay, how often, when was the first repayment?'

'Started in January and it was the maximum we could find, five hundred a month. Then the fourth time I went to pay another month's amount, he . . . he said I wasn't to repay any more.'

She spoke shrilly. 'And now you're certain Tim's lying, aren't you, Inspector? You can't believe anyone could be so generous. And because he's dead, he can't . . . Oh my God!'

'What is it, Nell?' Kiernan asked.

'He's wondering if you or I killed him to avoid the debt.'

'For God's sake . . . Inspector, I'm sorry for that. My wife is very upset.'

She ignored her husband. 'He's a detective, trying to find out who did kill Robin. Would he give a damn about the IOU unless he thought it was significant? Can't you see that?'

'The inspector has said nothing about Robin's death.'

'No. So that we'd talk more freely.'

Alvarez spoke sadly. 'Señora, please understand it is my job to consider all possibilities.'

'You don't deny you're wondering if we killed him?'

'It had to be a possibility.'

'Had or has?'

'Did Señor Gill give you receipts for the repayments you made?'

Kiernan answered. 'No.'

'Since you had given an IOU, you did not think it might be an idea to have evidence of your repayments?'

'It seemed . . . If I asked for a receipt, it could be because I didn't trust him even after he had been so kind.'

'Did you repay by cheque?'

'He preferred cash.'

'What's that matter?' she said wildly.

'Señor's Gill's bank statements would have provided proof of the repayments.'

'And if there was that proof? You wouldn't think we might have killed him to prevent further repayments? You'd continue suspecting us. How I wish to God we'd never accepted the money; Tim was right to want to refuse it. Better to have slunk home and lived on charity than to be suspected of murdering someone who was so incredibly kind.'

A noble thought. But like most noble thoughts, either impossible, too illogical, or calling on too much self-sacrifice to be implemented. 'Mrs Kiernan, can either you or your husband tell me where you were at midday on the fourth?'

They looked at each other. Kiernan answered. 'We can't afford to do much, so we must have been here.'

'Have you friends or anyone who could corroborate that you were?'

'When time means so little, who's going to be certain enough for you to believe?' she asked.

Alvarez thanked them for their help and left, saddened by the certainty he had brought them fresh fear.

He sat at his desk and watched motes dancing in the broad shaft of sunshine. Had the Kiernans been telling the truth? Or did they think him sufficiently stupid to believe he would accept their story that they were lent, and later given, the remaining eight thousand pounds for no reason other than sympathy?

She was the driving force. If Gill had never cancelled the debt, would she have proposed his murder in order to get rid of a debt that remained difficult to meet and, as the cost of living rose, perhaps impossible?

He judged her to be an ordinary wife; ordinary wives, however strong-willed, did not plan murders. Yet would Salas accept his judgment? Of course not.

Accept the Kiernans had been telling the truth. How to prove this when there was an undestroyed IOU and no records of repayments? . . . Perhaps there could be a negative record . . .

He checked the phone number of the accountant who occasionally worked for the cuerpo and dialled it. A secretary said Señor Ibarra was very busy; after he had introduced himself, Ibarra was not too busy to talk to him.

They exchanged family news before Alvarez said: 'I want you to come along to Aquila and examine bank statements over three months of this year. It's important to know if there are signs of regular reductions until a short period when there was none.'

'When d'you want me there?'

'How about now?'

'Not possible. This afternoon?'

'It's Saturday.'

'You suggested this was an urgent matter.'

'But not priority.'

'Since I don't work on a Sunday, it had better be Monday, nine o'clock.'

'Ten. It takes time to drive up to the house.'

'Shall I pick you up on the way?'

'Thanks, but I can't be certain where I'll be before ten.' Ibarra drove a sports car with a long bonnet and the exhaust noise of a mad buffalo. He had won the local hill climb one year, crashed the next. The thought of being driven on roads edged with death by a would-be racing driver was worse than that of driving himself.

'A pleasure to see you again, Inspector,' Parra said.

A hint of mockery because he had intended to change his cotton shorts after he had spilled coffee on them, but had obviously forgotten? 'How is the señorita?'

'Perhaps a little better. She will be glad to see you.'

Parra's regular greeting. And probably to every other guest since he understood the art of making one feel one was of importance to someone else.

Mary was sitting on the main patio, in the shade of a sun umbrella. She smiled her greeting. 'Your arrival gives me the excuse to put down this book and shut it.' She placed it down on the patio table. 'I was told I must read it by the literary lioness of the village, who boasts of having read *Remembrance of Things Past* in the original. She called yesterday to pry and gave the book to me because it had won a prestigious literary prize. There's nothing on the cover about a prize, but it's sufficiently leaden to have won one . . . Why are you still standing?'

'I haven't been asked to sit.' He sat. Parra had been right – she was more cheerful.

'Now, Enrique, you can tell me why I'm being honoured?'

'Would you not prefer to say, hounded? I wanted you to know I'll be along tomorrow with an accountant. I've asked him to look through some of your uncle's papers. Hopefully, he won't be here long.'

'More problems?'

'I'm not certain. Just checking up to see if there are.'

'Sounds complicated . . . I do so wish it was all over.'

'I'm doing all I can.'

'As well I know. From the awful beginning, you've been a real friend. God knows how I'd have got through everything without your help.'

'It was nothing.'

'The standard Mallorquin answer to every thank you, which makes me think of false modesty . . . Damn! I've made it sound as if you're being falsely modest . . . A quick change of subject. Why haven't you said what you'll drink?'

'Because you haven't asked.'

'Which makes me a very poor hostess.'

'And me a very poor guest since I was wondering why I hadn't been asked.'

'Were you? We must set your mind at rest. Would you be kind enough to call Pablo? The button's there.' She pointed.

He pressed the call button set in a small piece of circular pottery in the house wall and returned to his chair. 'I've been meaning to ask you something.'

'Now it's confession time? You didn't come here to see me and tell me about tomorrow, you came to ask more horrible questions.'

'You misjudge me.'

Parra came out on to the patio. 'Yes, señorita?'

'I'd like a lady's gin and tonic and the inspector will say what he wants.'

'Coñac with just ice, Inspector?'

'Yes, please,' Alvarez replied. Was Parra trying to show Mary how smart he was? Parra left. Alvarez said: 'What is a lady's gin and tonic?'

'Twice the tonic and half the gin of a gentleman's. Now you can tell me why I was misjudging you.'

'By inferring I wouldn't have come here unless I had to.'

'If there were no questions, you could have phoned and told me about the accountant.'

'Which would have meant my missing this meeting.'

'You don't fool me. You've a so-far undeclared reason. All right, what are the questions?'

'At the time, did you know your uncle was lending the Kiernans a considerable sum of money?'

'I did. He mentioned them one day, said he thought they were a very pleasant couple who were in a nasty financial mess. What did I think of his lending them enough to pay off their mortgage? I said, do it.'

'Did he later tell you he had done so?'

'No.'

'Did he mention that after they'd repaid him a little of the money, he told them not to repay any more?'

'No. And you sound kind of disbelieving. About the gift or the secrecy? As for the gift, Robin was a very generous man, as I've every reason to know. He liked them and was happy he could help them. As to my not knowing, one of his favourite slanders was that a woman's tongue proved perpetual motion was possible.'

'But he never confirmed that he had made them that gift?'

'Why do you keep asking?'

'Because as I told you, the IOU is still in the safe.'

'He'll just have forgotten to tear it up.'

'He could be that forgetful?'

'By his account, no, by mine, yes.'

'And a gift of that quantity doesn't surprise you?'

'It obviously does you . . . For me, it does not, not, not!'

Parra came out of the house, tray in hand, as she spoke. 'Is something the matter, señorita?'

'Merely expressing my negative opinion in triplicate.'

Parra put glasses and a bowl of cheese straws on the table, and returned indoors. Alvarez picked up his glass. 'Do you know the Kiernans well?'

'Reasonably so. Nell has more in her head than most wives out here and possibly will even be able to enjoy reading this.' She touched the book. 'If she can help someone, she does. Which is why it was great that Robin was able to help her.'

'What about Timothy Kiernan?'

She began to revolve her glass between first finger and thumb. The ice clinked against the side. 'It's become the expat's habit to kiss on both cheeks when meeting a female friend. I could never nerve myself to let him, so he gained the impression I disliked him. I couldn't find the courage to explain.'

'Would you consider him in any way a violent man?'

'In every way, it's no, no, no again. It's Nell who wears the trousers and fights with authority.'

'Could she be violent?'

'You do have a very strange mind and I don't think I'd like to look inside it.' She drank. 'That's being rude again and I didn't mean to be.'

'I have to consider many strange possibilities in order to discard them.'

'Why on earth think either of them could be violent? Or are you wondering if . . .' She spoke sharply. 'If you're thinking either of them could have hurt Robin, you're sick!'

He soon left. The warm friendliness, her newly found carefree manner had disappeared when she had guessed the reason for his questions.

He parked in a forbidden space in the old square, left his car and crossed to Club Llueso. Roca noticed him enter, poured a drink and brought it along the bar to where he stood. 'You look like you've been kicked where it hurts. So I've poured a double double. But don't let on or you'll have me sacked.'

SIXTEEN

'I've often wondered what this place is like,' Ibarra said as he stood by his car and gazed at Barca and beyond. 'A Mallorquin Mount Olympus.'

It was to be hoped the gods did not suffer from vertigo, Alvarez thought. 'I want to check I made myself clear over the phone and you understood me. Señor Gill may have been paid fifteen hundred euros during the three months before his death. There's no written record of this and there was only a relatively small amount of cash in the safe. I'm wondering if there was a break in regular withdrawals from whichever bank he used to cover the costs of running this place which could suggest he was briefly in receipt of an extra income in cash.'

'Difficult unless he withdrew weekly, or fortnightly, to meet staff wages and house costs.'

'I think he was a man who would have done so.'

'We'll find out.'

Parra opened the front door. 'Good morning, señors. A welcome fine, sunny day.'

As it had been for weeks, Alvarez silently and sourly commented. Soon, there would be the first rain. What would Parra's greeting be then? A welcome rainy day? 'Is the señorita in the sitting room?'

'She has asked that you go up to the late señor's library and carry out whatever work it is you have to do.'

'I'll say hullo first.'

'The señorita has said she does not wish to be disturbed.'

'She is ill?'

'As far as I know, she is well.'

Parra had spoken without his usual assumed deference. Because he was aware that the inspector's departure the previous evening had been a shamefaced one? People with small minds liked to see authority mocked or denied.

'Will you need the keys to the safe, Inspector?'

'Yes.'

'Then I will hand them to you.'

'You have them?'

'The señorita handed them to me before your arrival. She will be grateful if you will return them to me before you leave.'

They went into the library. Alvarez swung back the section of bookcase, unlocked the safe, brought out bank statements and paying-in notices, and placed these on the desk. Ibarra had been looking along the lines of books. 'A well-read man.'

'I imagine so.'

'Most of these have obviously been opened and read, unlike those in many private libraries, there to impress.' Ibarra turned round. 'Is everything ready?'

'I think so.'

'One point you haven't covered is whether you want my report to be ready for the court?'

'That would be best.' Since Ibarra would have to do the work, it seemed more reasonable to be prepared for all possibilities.

He was becoming concerned they would not be leaving in good time for lunch when Ibarra crossed to where he sat. 'There's reason to accept he was paid largish sums in cash on three occasions, at monthly intervals.'

'I'm glad.' Which was a ridiculous thing to say since, as he immediately recognized, once again a theory of his had been proved wrong.

He returned everything to the safe, and locked it. They left the library, he crossed to the sitting room and went in. Mary was watching the television. 'I have the safe keys . . .'

'Will you return them to Pablo, please.'

'You'll be very glad to know . . .'

'I'll call him, so that he'll be waiting at the front door and you won't be delayed in your efforts to blacken more innocent people.' She depressed a bell push by her side.

He left.

*   *   *

Alvarez spoke over the phone. 'I am just back from Aquila, señor.'

'Interesting. But it would be far more interesting had you remembered to explain why you were there.'

'After I had questioned Señor Kiernan, who signed the IOU which is in the señor's safe . . . .'

'Why and about what did you question him?'

'I suspected his IOU provided the motive for Señor Gill's murder.'

'Did it?'

'On the contrary.'

'He was able to offer an explanation of events which you had to accept?'

'Señor Ibarra has checked the bank statements and other figures . . .'

'Who is Ibarra?'

'You know . . .'

'Who is Ibarra?'

'The accountant we employ when there is accountancy work which needs to be carried out. He went through all recent figures and there was evidence of three months during which the normal amounts in cash had not been withdrawn from a bank.'

'That is important?'

'Señor Kiernan claimed he had three times repaid five hundred euros . . .'

'You will stop there and start again. If I am to understand what you are saying without having to ask constantly for elucidation, you will explain why you were doing what you did, what you learned from Señor Kiernan, whether he was able to provide an alibi, or whether you still believe there is cause to believe him guilty of Señor Gill's death.'

Alvarez made a full and detailed report.

'You no longer believe him to be guilty?'

'No, señor. I mean, yes.'

'You would care to choose between the two possibilities?'

'No, I no longer believe him to be guilty, yes, I no longer believe him to be guilty.'

'There are times when I wonder . . .' Salas stopped. 'You have questioned the staff again?'

'Yes, señor.'

'And are satisfied none of them had any part in the señor's death?'

'Their alibis show none of them was near Aquila at the time of the señor's death.'

'You have discovered, uncovered, or fantasized further unusual motives?'

'No.'

'Then you can offer no further suspects'

'That is so.'

'Did you express the view that there is an advantage to be gained from proving a suspect's innocence because it eliminates him? Now that you have eliminated your last suspect, would you like to explain that advantage more fully?'

'It shows the señor's death was an accident, not murder.'

'Since, despite the findings at the inquest, that was always the more likely verdict, it seems you have conducted a long and unnecessary investigation.'

'I don't think that's so.'

'To start from a verdict and spend weeks returning to it is an example of extraordinary ineptitude.'

'But for my work, there could be no certainty that, since no one had the motive to murder Señor Gill, his death was an accident.'

'You would claim that to be logical?'

'Yes, señor.'

'When you have made a gross error?'

'I don't see that I have.'

'You have refused to listen to your senior's advice.'

'Are you going back to . . . Are you suggesting . . .'

'I am referring to Señorita Farren. From the beginning of this investigation, she has been the prime suspect since she had more to gain from her uncle's death, the greatest opportunity to encompass it.'

'Impossible!'

'You find it difficult to follow your own logic? Motive

was the key, those with motives had to be suspects, when all but one suspect is found to be innocent, the guilt of the last becomes certain.'

'Señorita Farren was so shocked by her uncle's death, she could not have had any part in it.'

'As I have previously pointed out, you are determined not to acknowledge a woman will always use her emotions to confuse a man.'

'Unless she is a superb actress, Señorita Farren's bitter grief was completely genuine.'

'You have proof she has no acting talent?'

'Of course I don't.'

'Then you cannot make such judgment. She has been left an estate which can be described as a fortune. Men will flock around her and she will choose whichever one will cause the greatest jealousy amongst her women friends.'

'She doesn't like men.'

'Then she will enjoy claiming the attention of women.'

'That's an unfortunate statement.'

'What the devil do you mean?'

'You're making the suggestion she is a lesbian.'

'How dare you make so abominable a remark? I would never refer to any woman in such terms.'

'The way you spoke . . .'

'Was without the slightest objectionable inference.'

'She does not like men because . . . She asked me never to repeat what she told me. If I were at liberty to explain, you would understand what I say.'

'You are too optimistic. Carry out my orders. Failure to do so will be treated as gross insubordination. You will treat Señorita Farren as prime suspect of her uncle's death. You will question her at great length and in the greatest detail. If she has an alibi, you will treat it as a lie. You will determine the relationship between her and her uncle.'

'I have done so and every single person stated without reservation there was a warmth between them which named a very close relationship. How could she even think of killing the man who came to her rescue when her parents were killed in an accident . . .'

'You will closely investigate any suggestion of a rift, however small, between them. And you will do so, aware that by your own logic, she is guilty of her uncle's death since she is the remaining person with a motive. Do you understand?'

'Yes, señor, only . . .'

'I do not intend to listen to any more emotional nonsense.'

'I was going to say, I am not sure how long it will take because . . .'

'Less time than you would like.'

'Because she's become reluctant to speak to me.'

'Understandable. Do you need to be reminded how to deal with a suspect who refuses to cooperate?'

'I can't bring her to the post and treat her like a criminal.'

'It has so far escaped your notice that that is how she is to be treated by you? Why is she refusing to speak? Have you made lewd comments which have annoyed her?'

'She was upset I could believe Señor Kiernan might be guilty of murdering her uncle.'

'It was your duty to believe him guilty, however mistaken the reasons for your belief.'

'She couldn't understand that.'

'Yet again, it seems you have made difficult what should have been simple. Nevertheless, however objectionable she finds your company, you will question her to the best of . . . I was about to say, the best of your ability, but for once you will make the effort to act professionally.'

Alvarez refilled his glass.

'You look as if she's finally found out where you live,' Jaime said.

'Why doesn't she know where Uncle Enrique lives?' Juan asked as he took the last of the baked almonds off the plate in the centre of the table.

'One does not ask personal questions,' Dolores said sharply. 'Nor does one take all the almonds.'

'What is a personal question?'

'You are trying to make out you do not understand me? What happens when you annoy me?'

'You get angry.'

'You now understand both question and answer. You can go out and play.'

'Isabel is out there with that stupid friend of hers. She tries to cuddle me, and the boys laugh.'

'Tell her you are too old to be cuddled like a child. Off with you.'

Juan left. They heard the front door slammed shut.

'It's sad that when one's young and is offered something, one doesn't want it, but when one's grown up, it's not offered,' Jaime remarked.

'You wish to be cuddled? Of course, not by me.'

'I was just thinking . . .'

'Your thoughts were with a nineteen-year-old with few, or preferably no, morals.'

'You think I'm interested in nineteen-year-olds?'

'When I am not there to observe you.' She turned. 'Enrique, you are not saying anything.'

'I have been ordered to do something which will cause great pain.'

'To whom?'

'To me and Mary.'

'The young person you have been seeing frequently?'

'Yes.'

'What have you been ordered to do?'

'Question her to know if . . . To prove she killed her uncle.'

'Could she have done such a dreadful thing?'

'Never. I'd bet my life on that.'

Jaime said: 'You'd need a better stake to interest anyone in the bet.'

Dolores spoke sharply. 'Must you constantly expose your lack of empathy with anyone but yourself?'

'When he says . . .'

She interrupted him. 'Enrique, you are clearly very upset about this woman.'

'I am.'

'Are you fonder of her than you have had us believe?'

'I thought you said a moment ago that one should not ask personal questions.'

'I was speaking to a child. Do I make a mistake to think of you as an adult?'

'Mary had a bitter life before she came to the island and it's been even worse in the past days. I cannot willingly add to her suffering; I cannot make it seem I believe her capable of an abominable crime.

'This morning, I had to suggest one of her friends might have caused her uncle's death. She became furious, like a genet defending her cubs. Her bitter anger, her terrible sorrow will be still greater when she understands I seem to believe she might be the guilty person.'

Jaime said: 'All you need to do is tell her you can't believe she did push her uncle over the cliff in order to inherit her uncle's money and live on the Riviera . . .' He stopped.

'You are thinking of the chits of girls with whom you like to imagine yourself,' Dolores snapped. 'Sweet Mary, my mother knew what she was talking about when she said a man had room for only two thoughts in his brain: food and women.' She spoke to Alvarez. 'The young lady was incensed you could suspect her friend and you are certain she could have had no part in her uncle's death, yet you have been ordered to treat her as if you believe she might have had?'

'Yes.'

'Then first you must regain her trust.'

'I doubt that's possible.'

'How typical of a man to admit defeat before he's begun. You tell her it was your fault you spoke in such a way she was bound to misunderstand you. It was obvious her friend could not have been guilty. Express deep sorrow at causing her so much grief. Tell her you have only returned to ask questions because that pompous and incompetent Madrileño has ordered you to do so. Left to yourself, you would never have bothered her again since not for one second have you thought she could have had any part in the tragedy. Frequently tell her you trust her implicitly. In all your years in the cuerpo, you have not met someone so patently innocent of any wrongdoing; to look at her is to know that if she found a hundred euro note in the street, she would hand it in to the police and make certain they traced the loser. You are questioning her when knowing her to be innocent, and your report will teach that mountebank Madrileño he is unfit for his job.'

There was a silence.

'Now I know why a woman's never in the wrong,' Jaime said as he reached for the bottle.

'You will drink no more,' she snapped.

'I've only had . . .'

'Far more than you should.'

Jaime showed unusual resistance. 'Since when has a wife had the right to dictate how much her husband drinks?'

'Since she made the mistake of marrying him.'

Alvarez drove ever more slowly up to Aquila, not from fear of the death-edged road, but because he did not wish to arrive. When Dolores had given her advice, it had seemed very positive; now he was not so sure.

He reached the house and braked to a halt. He opened the door and waited, he knew not for what – miracles had gone out of fashion. Parra left the house and crossed to the car. 'Good afternoon, Inspector.'

'Is the señorita here?'

'May I suggest you do not leave your car?'

'Why not?'

'I have been told you are no longer welcome in the house.'

'I have to speak to her.'

'I did not make myself clear?'

'Quite clear. So I'll do the same. I am going inside and speaking to the señorita and if you get in my way, you'll end up on your arse.'

'Is that a threat of violence?'

'Make of it what you will?' Alvarez left the car, pulled the door free of Parra's hand and slammed it shut, crossed to the front door, went inside.

Mary came out of the sitting room. 'Didn't Pablo tell you to go away?'

'He did.'

'Then would you please do so.'

'After you said what you thought of me last time, d'you think I'd be here now if I didn't have to be?'

She looked past Alvarez. 'Pablo.'

'Señorita?'

'Phone the police and say a man has broken into my house and I want them to come and remove him.'

Alvarez said: 'If the policia come here, Mary, it will be to take you to the village for questioning.'

'Oh, my God! You're threatening me now!'

'No. But my superior chief refuses to listen to reason.'

She turned. 'All right, Pablo. There's nothing we can do in the face of the bullying.'

'I will stay to make certain he does not molest you, señorita.'

Alvarez said, 'You will disappear quickly, or I'll have you arrested.'

'If you . . .'

'Pablo, please leave before the inspector enjoys the pleasure of trying to prove himself the big man he would like us to believe him to be.'

Parra left. She went into the sitting room and closed the door behind herself. Alvarez opened it and entered. 'Please try to understand, Mary . . .'

'Señorita Farren.'

'Of course it was ridiculous to think your friend, Señor Kiernan, could possibly have had any part in the death of your uncle, but I was ordered to question him to find out whether he had been trying to escape the repayment of the money he owed . . .'

'He owed nothing.'

'I knew that after speaking to you.'

'No. Only after the accountants had finished their work. Someone capable of any understanding would have known without their pawing through uncle's papers.'

'I hated causing you so much bitter distress.'

'You kept your emotions very well hidden.'

'You think I enjoyed upsetting you? I've said, I was ordered to make those enquiries.'

'And that justifies them? The Nazi war criminals tried to justify their brutalities on the grounds of orders. Most of them were hanged.'

'You'd like to see me hanged?'

'You have no room for the feelings of others, no sense of remorse for what you are doing. An order is an order.'

Contrary to Dolores' belief, his words had enraged, not pacified. 'You obviously want me out of here . . .'

'Pablo made it very clear I did not wish you to enter the house, but being a bully, you threatened him. Had he decided physically to prevent your coming in, you would, of course, have claimed his action could not be excused on the grounds of my order.'

'I'll leave as soon as I've asked something.'

'Is it which of my uncle's other friends should become the next suspect?'

'Have you remembered anyone you saw in Palma on the fourth who will remember the meeting?'

'You . . . You've come here to find out if I killed Robin. When I loved him for his kindness, his humanity . . .' Tears slid down her cheeks.

'Please try to remember someone,' he pleaded.

She spoke with difficulty. 'If it'll get rid of you. I was in Perfección. Buying a frock because Robin was going to give a special party and I wanted to look as nice as I can. Then when I got back home, he wasn't there and I just thought he . . .' She ran out of the room and he heard her hurry up the stairs.

As he walked to the front door and opened it, Parra appeared.

'I doubt you'll bother to come back, Inspector.'

On his drive down from Aquila, Alvarez did not once pay heed to the deadly perils he was facing.

SEVENTEEN

The phone rang. Alvarez reluctantly picked up the receiver and identified himself.

'The superior chief will speak to you,' Angela Torres said.

The way she had spoken suggested he was being granted an honour. It was one he would have happily rejected.

Salas spoke without any preliminary greeting. 'Have you questioned Señorita Farren?'

'I am recently back from having done so, señor.'

'Why didn't you get in touch the moment you returned?'

'When I said "recently", I meant I had only just done so.'

'It would be an advantage if you learned the recognized meaning of words.'

There was a silence.

'Do you intend to make a report?'

'It took me time and considerable effort to persuade the señorita to answer me and . . .'

'There is no reason to waste time over irrelevant details.'

'They were relevant at the time.'

'Why are you prevaricating? Is it because you allowed her to refuse to answer you?'

'I am trying to explain it was only by telling her it was your fault that I encouraged her to answer me.'

'What the devil caused you to make that ridiculous and incorrect allegation?'

'You had ordered me to question the Kiernans because they were suspects. Had I not made that clear and had personally believed the accusation to be ridiculous, she would never have given me the information she did. There has been even more trouble. You insisted she be treated as the prime suspect. When I arrived at Aquila earlier, the manservant tried to prevent my entering the house on her orders. However, I went inside and persuaded her that she

had to give me an alibi. That seemed to make it obvious
that I was now wondering if she had murdered her uncle.
She was deeply upset and . . .'

'Was she able to provide an alibi?'

'She had been in Palma, buying a dress in a shop called
Perfección. It is a very expensive shop, but ladies seem
willing to spend a great deal of money on themselves.'

'I am very well aware of that. My wife . . . Continue.'

'I spoke on the phone to the manageress and asked if
she could confirm the facts. She checked the sales' records
and on the fourth, at twelve thirty-five hours, Señorita Farren
bought a frock for four hundred and fifty euros.'

'Was it made of gold thread?'

'I don't think it's all that expensive by modern prices.'

'I believe you are not married. You will leave such inane
remarks to those who are.'

'She paid by credit card. The person who made the sale
could remember that the woman in question suffered from
a facial disfigurement. Despite your insistence that the
señorita was the prime suspect, there can be no doubt the
buyer was the señorita and therefore could not have been
responsible for her uncle's death.'

'Is it ignorance or incompetency which causes you to
refuse to consider the possibility she hired someone else to
carry out the actual murder?'

'That is as impossible as your naming her a suspect.'

'If that is so, has it yet occurred to you that everyone
whom you believed had a motive has now been cleared of
involvement in the death?'

'Yes, señor.'

'Have you conjured up further fantastical motives?'

'No, señor.'

'You still deny the possibility of suicide?'

'Yes, señor.'

'So have you come to any conclusion?'

'The señor's death was an accident.'

'My understanding was that you were certain it could
not have been.'

'With all the evidence . . . It did seem . . . The forensic

surgeon's findings were that although there were no signs of contact with the cliff face, it was possible the bruising could have been caused during the fall.'

'Was there not mention of a blow about which you have made great play?'

'Yes.'

'And the surgeon said it might also have occurred during the fall, but as there was no damage to the clothing, that did seem unlikely.'

'He didn't say "unlikely".'

'He understood your capabilities?'

'One can't always be right.'

'Yet on the contrary, one can always be wrong.'

'Señor, I could only . . .'

'Because I made the mistake of accepting your judgments, I allowed you to continue an investigation which has been a waste of my time and of yours. In the latter case, such waste is of little account.' Salas rang off.

There was satisfaction in completing a case, even when completion had produced only allegations of incompetence. No longer did he have to try to remember what he was supposed to have done and hadn't; whether there was inescapable reason to speak to Salas or the necessity of expecting Salas to be in touch with him. He could take a little longer to enjoy his *merienda*; he could steal those few extra minutes for his siesta which were more valuable than those which had gone before.

'It's good to see you smiling once more,' Dolores said as they ate.

'Life is once more bearable with the case over and done with.' He refilled his glass.

'And the niece was not as nasty as you expected?'

'Not . . .' He remembered. 'She was not, because I carefully followed your advice.'

'Bet she thought you were overdoing things,' Jaime said.

'You are implying something?' she asked sharply.

'It did seem you wanted him to lay it on with a trowel.'

'Naturally you would think that, since you are unable to

understand a woman needs kindness, the occasional word of praise, an appreciation of how she sacrifices herself for others.'

'If I started to talk to you as you said he was to do to that woman . . .'

'Your words would be intended to hide your refusal to do as asked or I had discovered what you had not done.'

'Wasn't Enrique merely putting up a smokescreen?'

'You cannot understand what I am saying because you have difficulty in considering anyone but yourself.'

'Doesn't matter what I say or do, I'm in the wrong.'

'That is true.' She spoke to Alvarez. 'Do you have to see her again?'

'No, thank goodness.'

'Why do you say that? I thought you liked her.'

'The relationship has entered the deep freeze. Further, every time she sees me, inevitably she's sharply reminded of her uncle's death.'

'She must be suffering greatly.'

'When she has a few million euros in the bank?' Jaime asked.

'Spoken like a man! If you win El Gordo this Christmas, I can be certain I will become of no interest to you since money will provide you with so much more than I can.'

'You know that's not how it is. You twist everything I say. I couldn't live without you. I wouldn't know how to continue. I would be dead while I was still living.'

'You wield a trowel too heavy for your strength,' she snapped.

Salas had not rung since Monday, not even to complain because he had not received the written report on the fatal accident suffered by Señor Robin Gill on Barca. Eventually, Alvarez acknowledged, he would have to draw up that report, but it seemed nothing was lost by leaving it until tomorrow.

He sat back in the chair and rested his shoes on the desk. Saturday was not long away. Then, he would enjoy the pleasure to be gained from letting the world slide by.

The contemplation of a forthcoming pleasure could be almost as pleasurable as the pleasure itself. Provided no major case suddenly disrupted everything, he would slide away from work a little early, have a coñac at the Club Llueso and return home for a drink before lunch. It was too hot for a heavy dish so perhaps Dolores would cook Riñones en salsa. Popularly not thought of as a grand dish, but in her magical hands it became one. Then a siesta, whose boundaries would not be limited by the need to return to work. In the evening, meeting old friends in Club Llueso. Dinner at home. Bacalao a la riojana? Dried cod, chorizo, onions, tomatoes, pimientos, pepper, olive oil . . .

The phone rang.

'Tollo here, Enrique.'

'Who?'

'You're the great inspector today? I'll remind you who I am. Not so long back, we took Matilde and Natalia to watch the Mar Déu del Arme, and it turned out you'd chosen the uncooperative one.'

'I remember nothing of the sort.'

'Convenient memory.'

'It's an offence to slander a member of the cuerpo.'

'It's a pleasure.'

'Are you still running a contract service for farmers?'

'What if I am?'

'I'll be along to make certain all your equipment is safe.'

'Not your job.'

'I'll have received a complaint and will call in a qualified inspector who will uncover many problems.'

'You can be a real sod!'

'We understand each other. Why are you ringing? What's your problem?'

'The wife is threatening murder, the husband has a lump on his head the size of a chicken's egg, and the second woman is having hysterics.'

'Call a doctor.'

'That's been done and if you don't turn up smartly, I'll tell your superior chief you were too tight to answer the call.'

'You're a bastard!'

'Like you said, we understand each other.'

'Where's the fun going on?'

'Aquila. Bit of an odd name . . .'

'Where?'

'Becoming deaf in your old age?'

'Who's having hysterics?'

'Someone said it was her uncle who fell off the cliff . . .'

Alvarez raced out of the room, down the stairs, past the cabo – who was astonished to see him moving quickly – out on to the street and along to his parked car.

A doctor was with Mary in her bedroom. Pablo had left in an ambulance. Luisa sat in the kitchen on the opposite side of the table to Alvarez.

'How could he?' she moaned yet again.

'How could he what?' he asked yet again.

She began to cry again.

He had tried to console her previously and had failed; there seemed no point in doing so again. He finished the coñac in the glass, poured himself another drink and added three cubes of ice from the ice bucket.

'We've been married seven years. You understand, seven years?'

There could be no sensible response. It was not a short marriage, not a long one.

'He always said a difference in ages meant nothing.'

It didn't when the woman was younger than the man.

'We lived in Lograsan.'

He nodded. He had no idea where she was talking about.

'It was so old-fashioned there was still a paseo. All the girls watched him because he was so handsome . . .'

He wondered why the doctor had not yet returned downstairs? Was Mary seriously ill?

'My parents were in a bus which crashed. I was their only child because that was what the good Lord had decided. They left me money and the house . . .'

He let his mind wander and only listened to snatches of what she said. Pablo had comforted her after her parents died . . . They had married . . . He had decided they would move from their ancient village and go to Barcelona where there was life. He had spent freely until there was nothing left of her inheritance . . .

They had come to the island because it was said to be easier to find work since there were many foreigners who were too lazy to do anything for themselves . . . She had been happy to work for Señor Gill and the señorita. But then she had not known Paquita lived nearby . . .

She had had no suspicions. Pablo had professed his love for her again and again . . . She had thought herself fortunate, even though she was a woman . . . That was until she found him with Paquita . . . She sobbed.

He wondered why it had never occurred to her that her husband, several years younger than she, who'd married her for her inheritance, would wander when there was no longer the money to hold him to her?

She had always done everything she could to please him. He had asked her to say he was with her that day. Of course she had agreed. A wife liked to please her husband. And how did he thank her? By bedding a puta . . . Heavier sobbing.

'What were you protecting him from?'

She ignored the question. 'I went to the pedicurist in the village in the morning because I have an ingrowing toenail. He was not there. His cousin had died, and he was at the funeral. I returned, went up to our bedroom to change my clothes and . . . He and his puta were on our bed. She covered herself as if ashamed, but she is a woman who has never known shame. I pulled her off the bed by her hair and said if she was not dressed and out of the house immediately, she would go out naked so all could see her for what she was.'

'You told me earlier that he asked you . . .'

'She went downstairs so quickly, she almost fell. Had I been near, I would have helped her fall. In the kitchen, Pablo called me names which I will not repeat. He demanded to know why I expected him not have fun with someone who could still give it. So I hit him.'

'With what?'

'The rolling pin which was on the table.'

The story contained the classical details of a marital break-up. But also . . . His imagination suddenly went into super-drive. Or insanity, as Salas would have it. 'You mentioned he had asked you to say he was with you, and because he was your husband, you had protected him . . .'

Wailing, she interrupted him. 'That he should take her to our bed and not one of the others!' Her body heaved from her sobbing.

He tried again to ask the same question. She shook her head in-between sobs.

'Why did he want you to say that?'

'I don't know.' There was resentment in her harsh voice; how could he be concerned with anything but her tragedy?

'Was it on the day the señor died?'

'Our bed!'

'He was not with you in the village that Friday?'

'She was with him in our bed!'

To suppose Parra had wanted her to support his false alibi because he had murdered Gill was to suggest he had done so without any motive apart from the small legacy . . .

Doctor Fechal stepped into the kitchen. 'I have done what I can for Señorita Farren, but unfortunately that was less than I wished. I wanted to make a brief examination in case there was a physical reason for her extreme emotional state, but she refused. She has also refused to take some pills which would help calm her. In such circumstances, there is nothing more I can do. If her condition deteriorates, get in touch with me. It may be necessary to take measures whatever her wishes.' He paused. 'You have my mobile number?'

'It will be in the phone book, doctor,' she answered.

Fechal left.

'I will go up and see if there is anything I can do to help,' she said.

'Would you rather I did, since you also are so distressed?'

'She is in her bedroom.' She left.

Men could never be trusted. He emptied his glass and poured himself a third brandy. Luisa returned. In tones of disapproval, she said: 'The señorita wants you to go up and speak to her. I have made certain she is decently dressed.'

He left and climbed the stairs. He had not asked which was Mary's bedroom and several rooms led off the corridor. He opened three doors before he found it. Mary, fully dressed, sat on her bed, supported by a pillow held against the backrest.

She reached out her hands and he went over, sat, held them.

'He . . . Pablo was with a puta . . . But he . . .'

'Let's talk about another trip to the bay . . .'

'I heard screaming and rushed to see what was the trouble. Luisa was threatening the woman with whom Pablo had been in bed. But . . . but . . . again and again he'd said he loved me from the day he came to work here. I told him not to be ridiculous. I liked him, but would never marry him. Robin would have been furious. Pablo went on and on, telling me that he couldn't bear to be without me, Luisa wanted to divorce him and he'd be free to marry me. I . . . I began to believe that at last there was a man who liked, loved, me for the person I was, who could make me ignore what happened in that garden in Ealing and I'd be able to mix with people and never flinch when a man touched me . . . Then I saw him with the naked woman and I understood he'd been secretly laughing at me for my naive stupidity. He didn't care about me. No one does. You're only kind to me through sympathy.'

'You couldn't be more wrong. Why do you think I'm here now?'

'Because I asked Luisa to tell you I wanted to see you. But you only came and saw me because it will make me believe you genuinely care about me. You don't. No one does. I'd be better off with Robin, dead.'

He had tried to make her understand she was not the outcast she believed herself to be, that betrayal did not damn the betrayed; she had every reason to face the world; her disfigurement was not nearly as great as she believed . . . But by what steps they had ended up on the bed, naked, was beyond him even as they lay side by side.

'Do you remember what I said to you?' she asked. She rolled over and rested her breasts on his chest. 'I told you, just friends. And you agreed. Another betrayal!' There was laughter in her voice. 'Are you going to marry me and make me an honest woman?'

'I will always honour you, always want to be your friend, rush to help you, but I will never marry you. I am old – I mean, older than you. You now know you are very, very desirable, you have no need to hide yourself, to be ashamed of yourself. Young men will flock around you and you'll choose the right one.'

'Marry me, Enrique.'

'And you won't stop wondering if it was you or the money which attracted me.'

'You're a fraud, scared of being tied down! But there's time for you to remind me what a strong husband you would be.'

'If you had come down any later,' Dolores said, 'you would be eating lunch, not breakfast.'

He sat at the kitchen table. 'I had to work very late.'

'Visiting all the bars?'

'There was trouble at Aquila.'

'Again? What was it this time?'

'The cook unexpectedly returned home to find her husband in bed with a puta. She thumped him so hard, he had to be taken to hospital.'

'One wife who remains a free woman! And how was the señorita?'

'Very upset, but I managed to calm her down.'

'How?'

'By persuading her that she was not the person she thought herself, that men would find her desirable.'

'It is to be hoped she believed you to be speaking genuinely.'

'I think she did.'

'Yes?' Salas said.

'In connection with the death of Señor Gill, I have learned

certain new facts which make it certain it was not an accident.'

'There were three possibilities, so I suppose one must be prepared for you to discount each one in turn and then start again. Do you intend to tell me what has caused this latest reversal?'

'It was because Luisa found her husband in bed with a puta.'

'To your great interest?'

'In her anger and emotional chaos, Luisa admitted she had been lying when I had questioned her. Parra was not with her at the time of the señor's death. He had begged her to lie about it and she had done so. The truth is, Parra murdered Señor Gill.'

'It escapes your attention that you have repeatedly claimed motive was the key element and that you rebutted the suggestion the legacy to each staff member was enough to constitute a motive?'

'The legacy was not the motive.'

'You are about to deliver a farcical possibility?'

'Logical, if unusual. Pablo decided he would marry Señorita Gill. She, as you will remember my saying, was in a highly emotional state when she came to the island, a result of which was she had the mistaken belief no one would wish to be friendly to her and if someone did, she was scared. Parra has a hair-oil charm and he cunningly engaged her emotions, said he'd been in love with her almost from their first meeting.

'She told him that it was impossible, that her uncle would never welcome their marrying. Pablo believed that if Señor Gill was so averse to the marriage, he would leave his wealth to her in such a way that he, Pablo, would not be able to touch it; or he might even disinherit her. There was one solution to the problem and this had the extra merit that, on Señor Gill's death, she would turn to him for comfort. He would probably have achieved success had he not made the mistake of entertaining a puta and being caught.'

'It is to be hoped few would have the vulgarity to refer

to "entertaining" in such circumstances or suggest his mistake was in being caught.'

'His wife was so outraged by his faithlessness, she hit him on the head and later inadvertently betrayed him to me. One could say, he was hoist by his own petard.'

'Only if one is of your persuasion,' Salas said angrily before replacing the receiver.